Duane Ivey is a traveling construction worker originally from Texas, and now hailing from Arkansas. He has traveled all over the country, and *Narrow Ridges* is set in a part of the country where he lived and worked for two years. He has always been a storyteller, but until now, has never ventured into the publishing world, and is looking forward to the adventure it entails. *Narrow Ridges* is his first novel.

To my family and friends; thank you for your support and patience.

Duane Ivey

NARROW RIDGES

AUSTIN MACAULEY PUBLISHERS™
LONDON • CAMBRIDGE • NEW YORK • SHARJAH

Copyright © Duane Ivey (2020)

All rights reserved. No part of this publication may be reproduced, distributed, or transmitted, in any form or by any means, including photocopying, recording, or other electronic or mechanical methods, without the prior written permission of the publisher, except in the case of brief quotations embodied in critical reviews and certain other noncommercial uses permitted by copyright law. For permission requests, write to the publisher.

Any person, who commits any unauthorized act in relation to this publication, may be liable to criminal prosecution and civil claims for damages.

This is a work of fiction. Names, characters, businesses, places, events, locales, and incidents are either the products of the author's imagination or used in a fictitious manner. Any resemblance to actual persons, living or dead, or actual events is purely coincidental.

Ordering Information:
Quantity sales: special discounts are available on quantity purchases by corporations, associations, and others. For details, contact the publisher at the address below.

Publisher's Cataloging-in-Publication data
Ivey, Duane
Narrow Ridges

ISBN 9781645369110 (Paperback)
ISBN 9781645369127 (Hardback)
ISBN 9781645369141 (ePub e-book)

Library of Congress Control Number: 2020910162

www.austinmacauley.com/us

First Published (2020)
Austin Macauley Publishers LLC
40 Wall Street, 28th Floor
New York, NY 10005
USA

mail-usa@austinmacauley.com
+1 (646) 5125767

Chapter One

The sounds of gunfire broke through the silence, echoing down through the valley and eventually, piercing through his subconscious into his conscious mind, causing him to immediately run for cover, as he had done so many times. His was a world where only the cautious survived. Sure it helped to be strong and fast with a gun, but without caution, no one survived very long. It was a wild land being filled slowly with wild men, who ran for the most part un-checked, able to do as they wished, until they ran into someone more wild than them. It was a time when the only law was in town, and they rarely ventured out, unless after someone who had wronged them or the town, they protected in some way that couldn't be left alone. But the towns in this part of the country were few and far between, which meant there would be no law around. So, once again Cabel Glaize would be left to his own devices to figure a way out of a situation that so far, he had no idea if or why he was even involved.

He had simply turned his horse into the tall scrub oaks that were next to the trail he was riding and stopped. He had learned through years of hunting and being hunted that the first thing that catches the eye is movement and he had no intention of catching the eye of anyone at this moment. The horse, he now rode, blended well with the country around him as did his clothes, already drab in color, they were now dusty and soiled from weeks on the trail. As he sat, he swore softly to himself realizing how close he was to his destination. This was not the way he wanted to begin his quiet ranching career.

He knew it wasn't him the shots were meant for or else he would already be dead or left dying in the trail like so many before him. He had never killed that way or cared for anyone who would, but he had no illusions about the kind of people that could be encountered during a man's life, even if it was short. Besides, this sounded more like a war. This was beautiful land, but not yet tamed and like the land itself, a lot of the new inhabitants were still wild and left to run at their own will. Short of the few renegades that were subject to break and run from the reservations from time to time, the Indian wars were over, but as anyone knew who traveled the country much at that time, the white man could be much more ruthless. The Indians had their beliefs that led them to do the things they were capable of; however, the white man could just be mean and he knew deep in his soul what was happening here. It could be Indians, but he would have heard if any had broken loose, for news of such things traveled fast these days, due to the severity of what a man might encounter out in the wilderness; no, these were no Indians, these were white men.

He had no idea who was doing the shooting or why, but he knew only a fool would go in there now and find out. Besides, it was none of his business anyway. He wanted only to be left alone, to find the place he was looking for. He had had enough of drifting and at the tender age of twenty-three, enough killing to last any man a lifetime. Now, here, he was nearing the end of the long journey that he and his brother had so wanted to make and walking right into the middle of a war or so it seemed.

Walking his horse on deeper into the brush, he slowly made his way through to the mountains that he had been skirting around for the past couple days. There were no real trails here, only those made by animals, but his horse was not long off of the range and took to the rough country as well as any. What he was looking for was a trail that led up into the mountains and to water and finding one, he took it. The wild animals all know where the water holes are, at any time, during the year, their lives depend on it, as much as a man's does. So, he followed the trail further up into the mountains. He was not necessarily in need of water right at this minute, however, it was not only common sense to camp by water but, also, to know where water was, if needed. But it was not only water he looked for, it was also land. He had come a long way to get to this part of the country, coming ahead of his brother, Dave, partly because he knew the trails better and what to look for and partly, to let his brother tie up some last-minute loose ends left from the death of their parents, only a few months ago. Now, he was here, where he wanted to put down the roots to start the new Glaize family, hopefully, without getting involved in the local conflicts that were apparently going on.

The shots had all died down by the time he found a good spot to camp. Nothing more than a little stream running out of the side of the rocks that over time had left a shallow cave, just big enough for him to sit. The front of the cave was nearly covered with a tangle of brush, so his small fire would be hard to see and being made with dry wood, there would be little smoke. There was no need in going to town today to let someone wonder what they had heard or seen, so he made his camp, stripped the gear from the blue roan, and after rubbing him down with a handful of grass, ground hitched him, allowing him enough room to reach the creek, at which, he had stopped. After tending to his horse, he boiled coffee and cooked the last of the food he had brought along with him for the trip. It was getting late in the year now and although the days were still hot, it cooled off considerably at night and at this altitude, it would be especially cool.

It was still early in the afternoon and being up high in the hills now, he would be able to see the country around him. It was a beautiful country with the mountains on either side, towering thousands of feet above him. It was late in the year and the colors in the high country were already starting to turn but the grass in the valley still shone green. This would be a good place to raise cattle. He had no idea of the place he and his brother had bought, but if it was like what he now looked at, he would be happy. He had not scouted his immediate surroundings, so he figured to have a look around, before turning in. After he had eaten, he eased further on up the trail to see if he could find a spot, in which, he could look over the country and by chance, see where the shots were coming from. His dusty clothes blended well with the trees and rocks that surrounded him, but being cautious, as a man, in the open country should be, he took the time to dig his moccasins out of his pack and slip them on his feet. He was not concerned about being seen by anyone that was not close to him, so he was able to maneuver himself into a position he could see most of the country to the north and west toward the town he was headed to. He could just see the outline of Willow Springs, maybe twenty miles to the west, and after that was all open country and then he noticed the trail of dust off to the north. Surely, they weren't coming for him; no one knew he was here or even on his way. He had told no one, other than his brother, of the route he would take or of the final destination. He had talked to a few people along the way in the various towns, but although he was and had always been friendly and easy to get along with, he was not one to divulge information that was not needed in conversation, so he had told no one. But, either way, he had a fairly large group of men riding fast in his direction. And judging the direction they were coming from, these were the same men who had been doing the shooting earlier. If they found him, they would be wondering what he was doing out here and if he knew anything about what had been going on, but even though he had not found the place he wanted, he was home now and this was no time to start being pushed anywhere. Also, there was a better chance the men knew where they were going and simply headed in the same direction to where he, now, sat. If that was the case, he may be able to learn a little about what was going on, given that he could find where they were headed. So, he hunkered down to watch and see what was about to unfold.

The riders were now coming up to the trail that he had been following, when he first heard the shooting start, but, so far, they were to the west of where he had turned off and with luck, they would cross his trail and not see his tracks. But he was never very lucky and one rider veered off to the east just far enough that Cabel knew if he was looking, he would see the tracks of a shod horse, leaving the trail abruptly and heading off into the brush and just as the thought came to him, Cabel could see the rider pull up and stop, then after a look around, called out to his buddies to come see what he had found.

"Well, okay, here we go, then. I should have known," he said aloud to himself, as he carefully worked his way back down to his camp to await what was sure to be some visitors shortly.

He saddled his horse back up, then brought it in closer and behind him, from where the riders would be coming and only after checking the loads in his rifle and six shooters, did he put on coffee to get ready to receive visitors.

Chapter Two

The land lay beautiful around here; the only sound was of the birds. Sarah had always enjoyed the early mornings out here. There was a peacefulness here that she had never before enjoyed anywhere she had ever been. She thought back through the years, since they had come to this country, and what a good decision it had been. Now, in her mid-forties, with the auburn in her hair slowly changing to grey and the twinkle in her eyes starting to be more of a reflection of the years, she wondered, what life would have been like had fate taken a different road for her. Not that she had any regrets; she just, sometimes, wondered how different life would've been, had they not come west.

The years had been good to her, especially so, since she had met Bob Sheah. He had come into town fresh back from the war in his Confederate uniform, proud as anyone could ever imagine. It had been one of those loves at first sight things that most people don't believe in, but believe or not, they each instantly knew they would be together forever. Wherever life took them from that day on, they had not spent more than a few nights apart at a time.

He hadn't been upset at the South's loss, like a lot of the soldiers were. Oh, he was a Southern man, all right, but he was also a realist and knew not only that, sometimes, things don't go as planned but also in some way, the South, for whatever their reasons had been, in a way, brought it on themselves. Or, maybe, it was just the restless spirit that has been born into every man, woman, and child who were lucky enough to have been born into these people who had made the journey and settled in this country that for so long was referred to as the new land. But, whatever the reason, he held no hard feelings toward the North and even complimented them, at times, on their ability to fight an enemy that was as cunning as the Southern army. He had always said, "I didn't join because I believe in what they're fighting for, I joined because it was my duty. Just as my duty is now to the United States, as a whole, and honestly, as it should be." He was a man with enough wisdom to see into the future; far enough to know that this country was better off fighting together than against each other and one day, the entire country would realize that.

They had come out here from Atlanta, shortly after the war, in an effort to escape some of the people, who did not look at things the way he did and with his views not being popular in the south at the time, they, together, figured it would be for the best. So, they sold what belongings they could not carry, loaded up, and came west into what they had figured to be a new start.

The first few years had been pleasant enough. They had settled on four sections of some of the most beautiful land she could ever have imagined. Then, shortly after Bob had used the money, they had to buy the beginnings of a herd. And now, with the herd growing and having just sold their first round of calves, trouble was brewing.

The Brantleys had recently moved into the area and they were a bad lot. It was easy to see what they wanted and that was everything. The main problem was they didn't want to earn it in the way everyone else did, at the time. They wanted land that was already cultivated, cows that were already producing, and women that either belonged to someone else or wanted nothing to do with them, such as her daughter Amanda. Yet, even as the thought came to her, she shuddered inside because she knew that her daughter had feelings for Tough Brantley. When around Amanda, Tough had shown himself to be a wonderful person; therefore, she would not even listen to the warnings; to stay away from him. Luckily, for the time being, he was scared, or seemed to be, of Bob, so he kept his distance. They would not have a chance to get together for some time, if things kept on the way they were. Besides, even though anyone that looked at Amanda had to agree she was a remarkably beautiful young woman. Sarah Sheah had the feeling that the only reason Tough was interested was because he and his father, Cobb Brantley, were out to get the ranch they had worked so hard to build.

Stirring inside the house brought her out of her daze and back to the real world, Amanda was up, and it was time to get started. Bob and the rest of the hands had gone to town for supplies, leaving her and Amanda there to do the things that had to be done. Bob had protested against this at first, saying that he would go alone, but she finally made him understand that they could get along fine here and that he may need the help, if trouble broke out on the trail. So, he had agreed, at last, to go but he left one hand here to help look after the place, just in case.

"How long is Pa supposed to be gone?" Amanda asked.

"He should be back in a few days," her mother replied.

Sarah answered her daughter's question, but she still felt the tension that seemed to be behind it. They all felt it. They all knew what kind of dangers lay in the twenty or so miles to Willow Springs. And they had all heard the shots. *"This was the worst of it,"* she thought to herself— the not knowing, the having to wait, until he was due back to find out if he's even still alive.

"G'morning, ma'am," Sandy Pearson's voice broke the silence that had settled between the two women, as they each sat with their own thoughts and worries.

Sandy was the lone cowhand that Bob had left behind to help out, until his return in case of trouble. He was a solid young man, in his build, as well as his manner. His name matched his appearance. He had a head full of sandy blonde hair, even more so now that it was in bad need of a cut. But, since the trouble had started, there had simply been no time. He was a young puncher from Texas, she had been told, that had seen nothing but hard times, since the day he found his way into this world; raised by his aunt and uncle, after Indians killed his parents, when he was only two. He had left there in a hurry, after his uncle, in a drunken rage, had beaten him. That was his uncle's last night on earth and Sandy's last night in Texas. He was only twelve, at the time. Sarah, sometimes, marveled that not only had the young man survived all this time, but that he learned all the manners and respect normally given to only the well-privileged. But when asked about it, Sandy's only reply was, "I just treat everyone as I would want to be treated. That's all."

He was a good boy and a good man to have around, when work started or trouble, for that matter, for, as Sarah had seen first-hand, he could more than hold his own, when the time came.

"Come on in, Sandy, breakfast will be ready shortly," Sarah called.

"Yes ma'am. Lost a few more head last night, ma'am. Rustlers again, I reckon. Trailed 'em for a ways. Headed off toward the Brantleys'. Oh, morning, Miss Amanda," Sandy had just noticed Amanda in the room.

Amanda was a lovely girl. Her dark brown hair had grown nearly to her waist and she had grown tall in the last few years. She was no dainty creature, for the years of growing up in this country had taught her the meaning of work and she was not one to be afraid of it. She had ridden with the herd, on more than one occasion and actually, found that she liked it. She was friendly and good-natured, but now her beautiful green eyes were growing red with fury, as she realized what Sandy was implying.

"And I suppose you want to blame the Brantleys right off of the bat too, right!" she tried to contain her anger but was not doing a very good job of it.

"Well, Miss Amanda, it's good to see you're well this morning," Sandy's voice was calm as always and that infuriated Amanda all the more.

"Why does everyone always blame the Brantleys first thing? Or is it just Tough you don't like?" Amanda argued.

"Look, ma'am, I just stated that the trail went off toward the Brantleys. Now, you have to admit how that looks. And this ain't the first time either and you know that, as well as I do. Now, I ain't accusing nobody, but if I was to start looking, that is where I would want to start."

He hated the thought of angering Amanda Sheah but one day, she would have to open her eyes and look around at what was going on. And, hopefully, before it was too late.

"You want me to go for a better look after I eat, ma'am?" Sandy asked.

"No, Sandy, we've got things to do right now. And with us being short-handed right now, it can wait," replied Sarah.

"Well, if it's okay, I'm going to go bring what I can on up here, closer to the house where they'll be easier to keep an eye on," Sandy said.

"That's a good idea. Amanda will go with you, Sandy," Sarah said, gesturing toward Amanda.

"Yes ma'am," Sandy agreed.

"Keep your rifle handy and hurry up. Just get what you can gather easy. We'll worry about the rest later," Sarah said.

"Will do, ma'am. And I wouldn't worry too much about those shots. You're married to one tough old man. It'll take some work to kill that feller," Sandy said, reassuring Sarah.

With that said and breakfast finished, Sandy and Amanda saddled up and left the house. It shouldn't take more than a few hours to get the biggest part of the herd, up to where they could be watched closer. It would be a help but as they rode out in silence, both had the same thoughts in mind. It would be good to get everyone together again. This thing was shaping up to turn ugly, before it was over and old man, Bob, was not going to be pushed out.

Chapter Three

The sun was already high in the sky, before they topped the last rise and looked down on the scene below them. Amanda knew she would never tire of scenes, such as this one. The main part of the herd, about three hundred head, was located in a large basin that was naturally fenced-in by the surrounding cliffs and bluff. Sure, the cattle could get out, if they wanted, but with good grass and water, it was not worth the effort it would take for them to leave. But the good grass also made it hard work to get them to move out. They were fat and lazy from the good grass and sunshine but with some effort, the two were finally able to get them moving.

Sandy was always amazed to watch Amanda work. There was simply no female in her, when it came to things such as this. But then, when not working, she was as dainty as any young woman he had ever seen. She was a vision of beauty, right then, though. Astride her buckskin, gelding with the sunlight reflecting off of her long brown hair, already covered in dust and sweat, working cows as well as most, any puncher could be expected. This was the type of woman he wanted. This was the type every man should want; strong, yet frail, at the same time. Not needing a man's protection, yet longing for it, as a woman should. But Sandy put the thoughts out of his mind, almost as soon as they came, for he knew not only that she didn't want him, but also that she did want Tough. For whatever reason, she had become infatuated with him.

These and other thoughts eventually seemed to run together, until he could no longer make sense of them anymore. The hard work and heat were starting to be the only thing on his mind. Most of the cattle moved along easily, but there was always some maverick or young heifer that didn't want to follow the plan and with only two people, it was a tough job keeping them all in line and heading in the right direction.

It was nearly noon, before they reached the valley, where they had wanted to leave the cattle. From here, they could easily keep an eye on them, without having to venture too far from the main ranch. There was enough work to do at the house, without having to ride two hours to check on the herd. Also, it was less likely anyone would come this close in an effort to rustle anymore.

The Brantleys were behind this. There was no doubt in Sandy's mind. He had not known them, before coming to this country but had seen their kind. They were a tough and ruthless lot. They wanted what Bob Sheah had, that was obvious, but it seemed like they wanted something else, too. Sandy had been thinking about this, when the first horse appeared. It had no rider. As it came closer, he recognized it immediately as the one that had been ridden by Tim Hickerson, when they had left the ranch yesterday and there was blood in the saddle.

Chapter Four

Cabel took a quick look around at his position and decided it was a good one. He had simply to roll to his left, from where he now sat and in two seconds, he would be completely invisible. The thought came to him that there were two sets of tracks in camp, one of his boots and one of his moccasins. The idea came to him so suddenly he almost had to laugh out loud. As quickly as he could, he shucked his moccasins and after hiding them in the brush behind him, he put his boots back on. He had just gotten this accomplished, when he heard them coming up the trail.

"Ho... the camp!" He heard one of the riders say.

"Come on in, if you're friendly. If you ain't, go away." Immediately, he reached out and ever so lightly, but loud enough to be heard, rattled the nearby brush with his hand.

He was not sure if they had heard it or not, but judging by the careful looks around, he had a feeling they had.

"Heard ya'll coming a ways back, so I put on some more coffee," he lied, knowing that the men had been as quiet as they could be. He just figured to give them a few things to think about, while they sat there.

Only three of the men in the group had come into the camp. The others, no doubt, had stayed behind to keep an eye on their horses and back trail. The third to enter was a wiry man of about forty-five. He looked vaguely familiar but Cabel couldn't be sure in this light. He had a dark complexion, with dark hair, trying to grey, with a handlebar mustache. He wore his pistols low on each hip, with the handles worn from much use and the thongs were loosened. Cabel knew this man but could not remember where from.

"Well, boys, look what we have here," The speaker, and obviously, the leader was a short man or short to Cabel's six feet three inches. Cabel guessed him to be in the neighborhood of five seven or eight. But what he lacked in height, he made up for in width. *"The man looked like a wall,"* Cabel thought to himself, with black hair, black as any Indian. His eyes were brown and ominous looking. The obvious smirk on his face showed the confidence, with which, he was used to operating. He had that confidence now, but it seemed to turn to anger, as he realized he was in front of someone, now, who was not shaken by him and obviously, just as confident. It didn't take Cabel long to decide he didn't like this man at all. He knew then and there that a fight was going to take place between the two of them, before he would ever find any kind of peace.

"I guess we've caught us a squatter. Fellers, what do you think?" The group laughed, but it seemed more out of habit than from the humor of the remark.

"Now, is that any way to talk to your new neighbor?" Cabel said amid the laughter that was coming from the men. Now, the mood turned more serious, for everyone knew that in order for anyone to move into this valley, they would have to go through the Brantleys.

"What's the matter, boys, you don't like company? Hell, I love a good barn raisin' every now and then," the smile was still on Cabel's face; however, there was no laughter in his eyes. For the first time now, the riders took a good look at the stranger they were talking to. Even though he was seated, his size was apparent, easily three inches over six feet, he also weighed in at an even two hundred twenty pounds. He had dark brown hair that was a mite too long and hung loosely out from under his weather-beaten, old hat. A few days' growth of a beard rounded out his features and put an even more sinister look into his ice blue eyes; eyes that would show fury, as well as laughter. And there was no laughter in them now. Also easily noticed, was his six-shooter strung low on his right hip and the way the stranger held his Winchester in his left hand. Kind of looked like it just grew there.

"Well, I guess we're about to get off on the wrong foot. I'm Cabel Glaize. Just come here from Virginia. How're you boys doing?" Cabel said, as he reached out in an effort to shake the leader's hand. Not trying to be friendly but wanting to feel the strength of the man, he knew he would eventually have to fight. But who was that third man? And would he get involved. He didn't seem to fit with this crowd. So, what was it? He had said nothing, yet, he had not laughed at Shorty's jokes either. Things here just weren't adding up.

"Your name has got to be Shorty."

It was the old deviltry coming out in him now. But it brought sudden laughter from everyone, even the third man, whom Cabel could imagine didn't laugh very much. The hard lines in his face were from squinting into the sun and dust out on the trail. And Cabel could guess this man had seen a sight of both. But who was he?

Not reaching out to shake hands, the leader glared out from under his new hat and replied, "My name is Tough Brantley and it would be in your best interest to remember that. We run this here valley, so, the best thing you can do is ride on, friend. You've no business here in Willow Springs and you'd best keep it that way."

Tough was mad now. He knew he didn't like this stranger and the sooner he was gone, the better.

"Okay, okay. I'll be moving on. Wouldn't want to stand in you boys' way," Cabel said, trying to sound as sheepish as possible. Still smiling, just to anger the little man even more.

"Good, that's what I like to hear…"

Then, before Tough could finish, Cabel added, "In about forty years or so, when there are too many people around here for my liking. But, right now, this is a beautiful valley and I think I'll stay."

Now even the smile on Cabel's face had been replaced with contempt. He was daring Tough Brantley to make a move. Cabel had known only a few men in his life that he really hated and, already, he knew he hated this one.

"I could kill you right here and no one would even know."

"You might. You might at that. But I'll tell you something, Shorty, you won't. You know how I know?

Because, I've seen a bunch of you idiots before now, and you're all just alike; full of talk, piss, and vinegar," he was on his feet, before anyone had realized it, "Now, you do what you think you need to, and you might get lucky and get me, but I'll get you, too. Make no mistake. And, my brother will take care of the rest of you."

"Your brother? Hell, there ain't nobody around us for miles. Except the Lawton boys, back down the hill," the new speaker was Blaine Derrick. A tough looking older man, with a don't-care attitude.

"You sure about that? I'm sure you've noticed the two sets of tracks around camp. And there's two coffee cups."

He had used one to cook his bacon, since he had lost his skillet a few weeks back. But just realized it was there, "Oh, Dave's out there all right. But you won't see him. You see, my ma died, when I was a baby. And, well, my pa pretty much lost his head and run off. Showed back up a few years later, sporting himself a Blackfoot squaw and a brand-new half-breed baby. Well, I always figured ol' Dave got a touch more of the Indian in him than he did the white man. Yeah, he's out there all right. Of course, if you don't believe me, go ahead and make your play. Be a hell of a way to figure out you were wrong, wouldn't it fellers?"

He was standing now and ready. Almost hoping someone would try him. He had been on the trail a long time now and was in no mood to be pushed.

"Blaine, get out there and find that breed," the boss' orders were simple, but Blaine didn't move.

"And I know a cave where a grizzly bear stays. I'll go in there tomorrow. How's that sound? Have you lost your mind? Go in the woods, in the dark, after a mad breed? You've gone plumb loco, Tough."

"Don't tell me you've gone yeller on me now, Blaine"

"Nope, I ain't. But I ain't gone stupid neither. You want that injun breed, you go get him."

With that being said, the big man turned and left the camp to head back to the horses. He had, apparently, decided it wasn't safe here anymore.

The anger was easy to spot now in Tough's eyes. He was used to giving orders and having them obeyed. Now, here was this stranger, from nowhere, who had not only defied him, but had insulted him in front of his men. And, in the process, cut into the order, in which, he held his men. This man would have to die; if not tonight, then soon.

"I don't believe you got no breed brother out there in the woods."

"You callin' me a liar now, Shorty? Why don't you throw down and find out? Don't tell me you've gone yeller on me now."

"Another time, Cabel Glaize. Another time."

The smile came back on Cabel's face, almost as if it had never left, "You boys want some coffee? I ain't had much company lately and I do love company."

Tough Brantley was mad clear through now and simply turned on his heel and walked out.

"Come on Slick, we need to go."

Slick! That was it, Slick Montgomery, the gunfighter from Missouri. But what was he doing here? And running with this rabble.

"No, Tough, I think I'll stay and have me a cup of coffee."

"Suit yourself, I'm gone."

After Tough had gone, Slick walked over and picked up the extra coffee cup, then walked over to the creek to rinse it out.

"Never did like bacon grease in my coffee," he said with a knowing grin.

"If you knew, why didn't you say anything?" Cabel asked, as he poured coffee for the two of them.

"Figured this one to be between you two. Besides, I never did cotton too much to Tough. It was good to see him put in his place for a change. Loved that part about your brother, too. Smoking Dave Glaize. Prizefighter, ain't he? Saw him fight once. That's one tough hombre, all right, but no more injun than I am. Know you, too, though, you may not remember. Arrested you one time down in Missouri; drunk and disorderly, if I remember right. Still drink, Cabel Glaize?"

Well, here, it was his chance to maybe find out what he had walked into. There was obviously some feuding going on here, but over what? Land? Water? There was plenty of both here, why would they be fighting over either of those.

"No, quit that night. Haven't had a drink since that night. Dulls the senses." Then after a moment of silence, he asked the question he wanted most to ask, "Just what in the hell is going on here, Slick?"

"Well, kid, it's the same ol' crap. It seems old man, Cobb Brantley, has settled a place south of here. Having problems getting a deed to it, though. Seems some easterner settled it before. Got a deed and all, and then hightailed it back east. Couldn't hack it out here, I reckon. Tried to track him down through the wire, but when they finally found him, he had sold the place. Won't say who he sold it to, though. Don't rightly know why, but he ain't talking no more. So, now, Cobb's got a burr under his saddle, says he'll not only own that place, but every place in the valley, before it's over. Right now, he's in a feud with old man Sheah. Sent some boys up there to talk to him today, but the old man apparently wasn't in a talking mood. I guess you heard the shooting."

"Yea, I heard it," Cabel said thoughtfully and then added, "You were a lawman, how did you tie into this?"

"Got into some trouble in Tucson, a while back. Had to take the outlaw trail, for a while. Not much cut out for it though. Thinking about getting shut of this bunch, before it gets any worse."

The two men sat quiet, now, for a while, each with their own thoughts. It was a good night to be out in the open, around the fire. The air had a little nip to it now, but it wasn't cold yet. Cabel had never been to Wyoming before this but had heard that it could get downright cold. So, this was a good time to be here, after the intense heat, but before the cold of winter set in. He had planned to have a herd in here before winter, but it didn't look good now. He would have a mess of trouble to clear up first. And Cobb Brantley was not going to be happy to learn who held the deed to the place he was now calling home. This was going to get ugly, before it was over.

"Hey, Slick, just a thought, but if you do decide to quit Brantley, I'll be needing a good hand."

"You?"

"Yea, you see, I know who has that deed that Brantley's been looking for. And," he added, "It'll give you a chance to get back on the right side of the law."

Cabel could see the wheels turning in Slick's mind now, as he thought about what had been said. Slick had been a good man in Missouri. What had happened in Tucson, Cabel had no idea, but he could not understand doing anything so terrible that he would turn full fledge outlaw.

The sudden realization of what Cabel had said brought laughter to Slick's eyes, like he hadn't had in years.

"You've got to be kidding me. Boy, you are fixin' to stir up a whole heap of trouble. Do you have any idea how old man Brantley's going to react, when he finds out you have the deed to his land? Man, when you enter a fight, you go in feet first."

"I didn't intend on entering one, when I left Virginia."

"Well, enter one, you have. That old man is gonna blow a lung, when he finds this out. I'm tempted to get out of it all together, just so's I can sit back and watch."

"Look, Slick, I know you're not an outlaw, as well as you do. You know the layout around here and I don't. I need you to help me straighten all this out and you need me to help you get straightened out. That sounds like a pretty good partnership to me, what do you say?"

"I say you're plumb crazy walking in here like this. But there's something about you that tells me you might just pull it off. Yea, count me in."

"Good, it'll be good to have you along."

After shaking hands, the two men parted, agreeing to keep their new partnership quiet for the time being. Slick was going to quit the Brantleys but keep the reason simple for the time being. For they all knew, his background was on the other side of the law and that he wasn't comfortable with the things he was involved in. His only hope was that Cobb would understand or, at least, let him out, without trouble.

Alone now in his camp, Cabel had time to think and plan. He had an ally now that knew the area and what was happening. So, his next move would be to get into town and hopefully, send a message to Dave, warning him of what was going on. Then he would have to have a good look around. He must locate his ranch, as well as the Sheah ranch. He must find and meet Bob Sheah and he would possibly have another ally. And from the sound of things, he would be a good one to have. These and other things were still running through his mind, as he drifted off to sleep. His first day in the area and he was already making enemies. What a way to start a new life.

The rising sun was just breaking over the horizon, when his eyes opened. At first, he lay still, letting the new sounds filter through. He could hear all the normal sounds one would expect to hear in the Wyoming wilderness, but nothing that sounded out of place. His horse stomped restlessly; eager to be back on the trail, so he arose and started his coffee.

After saddling his horse and packing most of his gear, he sat down for a cup of coffee to think. He, now, knew what the feud was about and, also, like it or not, he was not only right in the middle of it, but was basically the reason for it. He was going to have to work carefully to get through this one. There was no way to get through, without a fight, he knew that, but, maybe, he could think of a way to minimize the fighting. That would be something to work on.

Even though he and Slick had not talked about it, he knew that nothing would be said to Cobb Brantley about the deed. He would find out, of course, but that would have to come in time. He did not have the deed. His brother would be bringing that out, when he came, so there would be no way, yet, that the Brantleys could get their hands on it. However, if they knew Dave would be bringing it, they could lay in wait for him. This worried Cabel, as he sat and thought. Of course, he would try to get a telegram out to warn Dave of the impending trouble, but there was always the chance he wouldn't get it. Or that the Brantleys would simply lay in wait and ambush him, out on the trail, somewhere away from here. If they were able to get their hands on that deed, they had simply to show up with it. They would have to make up a story, of course, of how they had gotten it, but Cabel had no doubt, whether or not the Brantleys would be able to dream up something. From what he had gathered from Slick, they were well-thought of here, so there would not be much of an inquiry. He had to come up with a discreet way of making them think he had the deed.

However, first things first, and mounting his horse, he rode back down to the trail he had been following, when he first heard the shooting start. The shooting! That was it. Slick had said that the party from Brantley's ranch had a run in with Bob Sheah and a couple of his boys. Did anyone else know it? Was anyone coming to check to see how the Sheahs had made out?

"Well, now, I know where to start boy. Let's go."

With a starting point in mind, he pointed the road west, along the trail he was riding. There had been very little wind and no rain, so he should have no problem finding the tracks of the men he had met last night.

The trail was easy enough to find and follow. It didn't appear these men were too concerned about someone finding them out. Although, in this country, normally, the wind blew all the time and the attackers must have figured their tracks wouldn't last in the wind.

He was moving north now, toward another range of mountains. Although they weren't as high as the ones south of here, they were just as beautiful and dangerous, for somewhere up there Cabel guessed, there would be men dying or maybe, already, dead. He had hoped to find the Sheah party in not too bad of shape, but he was a realist and was prepared for the worst.

The tracks were joined here by another rider, coming from the west. So, that would be why Slick acted, as he had no idea what all had had taken place in the fight. He wasn't there. That was good to know. At least, he hoped it was Slick and given the man's background, Cabel did not think the man would stand by and watch an innocent party be murdered, let alone participate.

So, Slick had been in town and missed out on the raid. Had that been on purpose? Cabel supposed it was. He was sure that the Brantleys would be smart enough to keep Slick out of things like that. At least, until they were sure the man was an outlaw and not still with the law.

He was coming into the mountains now, so every step would have to be made with caution. If anyone was still alive up there, they would be wary of anyone coming their way. He was close now. He could tell by the tracks of the horses. They had been running, when they came through here and had slowed to a walk, after they had gotten on into the valley.

There was a good chance he was within rifle range, now. Hopefully, these men wouldn't shoot first and ask questions later. But that was a risk he would have to take. He knew there might be men up there, somewhere dead or dying. If they were dead, someone would want to know. If they were dying, well, that could be the most dangerous. A dying man has nothing to lose.

Chapter Five

"Bob, you seeing what I'm seeing?"

Will Kollet was only nineteen but had already seen more than most folks twice his age. His life had been filled with a wonder of who he was and where or if he belonged. Raised by adopted parents, he had barely known his father and his mother, not at all.

Will had killed his first man, during an Indian attack, shortly after leaving home. The attack was almost over, before he made it close enough to see what was happening, so he had hid out in the brush and waited. There had been only four Apaches there that day and three are still there, unless the one survivor carried them off, as Indians were subject to do. But Will didn't believe he had, for he had looked into the Indian's eyes, he was hurt badly himself. The Indian had fallen to the ground and Will had walked up to him with the intention of killing him.

"No, I'll wait. You might die here for the buzzards to feed on. But know this injun; if you live, the next time you look into these eyes, you will die. As God is my witness, you'll die."

He had no idea, if the Indian had lived or not. He simply walked away and never looked back. He had lived from town to town, shining shoes or mucking stalls. Doing anything he could to survive, until he had met Bob Sheah, who had taken him into his family and treated him like his own son. And Will felt the same way. He would kill or die, just as easy for this man as he would, if his own father were still alive. Now, here, they were, in the blazing heat, bleeding, and probably, dyeing from a fight they had not wanted, watching a lone rider ease closer and closer.

"Yeah, Will, I see him."

"Any idea who he is?" Will asked.

"Nope, never seen him before. Might be someone Brantley hired new. Or it might be somebody, just stumbled in."

"I can take him from here, if you want."

"No, let him be for now. Let's just see what he's up to."

Bob Sheah had seen enough needless killing in his lifetime. He knew most everyone who worked for the Brantleys, but this man he had never seen. It might be that he was just someone wandering through and stumbled into this mess. But, no matter, he was going to give the man a chance to explain his business here, before the shooting started.

Cabel had found where the attackers had tied their horses and went in closer on foot. Here and there, a smudge or mark on rock or a broken twig, told the way each man had went. Here, is where, they split up. The one with the little feet, probably Tough, had went left here, up between the rocks. Cabel dismounted and followed the trail, until he, eventually, found where the man had waited, apparently for some time, by the cigarette butts lying on the ground. One thing, for sure, was clear; these men weren't worried about being found out. Anyone in the country could have followed their trail.

Below, he could see the buckboard, right where it had probably stopped, when the attack began. It was still intact, although the horses had been killed. The men from the Sheah ranch were nowhere in sight, however, so Cabel, going back the way he had come, made his way down to the wagon.

"Hold it right there, young man."

The voice had come from behind and to his left. It sounded like the voice of an older man, so Cabel spoke.

"You'd be Bob Sheah, I reckon," Cabel guessed.

"Yeah, that I would. Who's askin' and how'd you know?"

"Name's Cabel Glaize. And I had a little talk with the Brantleys last night myself."

"Right friendly with them Brantleys, are you, son?"

"Mister, to the best of my knowledge, I ain't got a friend in this valley. But when five armed men come into my camp, I tend to get conversational, if you know what I mean?"

"Well, what are you doing up here? They paying you now?"

"No, sir, just thought maybe you and some of these boys might be hurt and in need of some help and maybe, talk a little business, if you're willing. Now, can I at least turn around?"

"Go ahead and turn, Cabel Glaize, but know this, you've got one of the best rifle shots in the country aimed at your guts. One wrong move and it's all over. You understand all that?"

"Yes, sir, I got no problem with that."

Cabel turned, then, with arms raised high, looking for the man whom he had hoped to befriend. When, finally, they emerged from the rocks he was not disappointed, for this was a fighting man, if he had ever seen one. He had no doubt, now, that had he moved, he would have been gut shot and left to the buzzards.

"If it's business you got, I'll save you the trouble, I ain't selling."

"Don't want you to. I've already got a place. About thirty miles south of here, deeded and all."

"South of here?" The old man questioned, "The only place I know of would be the Brantley place. And deeded, you say?"

"That would be it. And yes, sir, it's deeded."

"Where did you get it?"

"Bought it from a man name of Williams, back in Virginia. Said he settled the place ten, twelve years ago, but changed his mind, after a couple years. Something about the winters being too cold."

"Yep, that's Williams alright. Good man just don't care much for cold weather. Can't say as I blame him, though. Might have quit myself, if I had anything to go back to. Aw hell put your arms down. We need your help, if you're willing. Got one man down in pretty bad shape, too. Gonna die, if we don't get him home soon. Where did you park your horse?"

"I'll go get him. He'll pull that wagon, if you can rig a single tree, out of that double."

"Well, hell, I know that. You just go get your horse."

Within minutes, the four men were loaded in the wagon and headed east.

Bob Sheah wasn't that old, being in his mid to late forties, but he had seen a lot in his years. And it was obvious, once you started talking to him. But, it was also obvious he was a good man, who cared about his employees.

Cabel glanced at the young man in the back of the wagon. He was in bad shape. He had been shot through the side. The wound had been cleaned with water, but was still bleeding, which, sometimes, was a good thing. The bleeding helps keep the infection out. But it wasn't going good for the young man now.

As Cabel looked at the young man, he realized that his appearance didn't fit in with his situation. He was a man of about twenty-five, with a smooth face. His round glasses gave him the studious look that kept him from fitting in.

"His name is Tim Hickerson," the old man had caught Cabel's puzzled look, "He showed up here a few years back and started up a newspaper. Was doing quite well with it, too, for no more than goes on around here. Then, one day, a traveler was found dead out, behind the saloon in town. And, well, Tim wrote a story on it. Next thing you know, his rent on the building was canceled. Now, I can't prove it, but I figure Cobb Brantley had something to do with it."

"How do you figure that?" Cabel was not only interested in the story but was thinking of the possibility of a story himself.

"Well, son, Cobb Brantley has his hand in a lot of things around here. Also, out here, we don't hardly worry what someone was before, but Cobb seems to know an awful lot about folks, that landlord, in particular. I think Cobb has something on that man he don't want anybody to know. And, I think, Cobb or his boy, more'n likely, had something to do with that dead man. And didn't want the story getting out."

"What happened to his printing press?"

"I let him store it in the barn at the house. He goes out there every few days and cleans it up. You know, knocks the dust off of it. Says he's gonna get it going again. I guess we'll see, if he makes it through this."

They were coming into the yard now. The first person Cabel laid eyes on was Amanda Sheah. And although there was much to do, he could not take his eyes off of her. He watched, as her eyes went from the horse pulling the wagon to the men inside and finally, on him. There, she paused for an instant. Or did she?

Sarah Sheah had come out also, when they heard the wagon pull into the yard and it was she who spoke first.

"What happened, Bob? Are you alright?" Sarah cried, as she saw the shape of the men in the wagon, "Is that Tim? Oh Lord, what happened, Bob?"

She was still asking questions but had already taken Tim out of the wagon and started for the house.

Amanda had not spoken through the entire ordeal. She had simply acted. She was strong, this girl.

"I assume this is your horse?" She asked to Cabel, once Tim had been taken inside and Cabel had started to unhitch his blue roan.

"Yes, ma'am, it is."

"Then, I owe you my gratitude for bringing my father and friends home. I am Amanda Sheah. And you are…"

"Name's Cabel Glaize, ma'am. Pleased to meet you."

For a time now, they just stood there, each thinking about the other, with neither knowing what else to say. Cabel had never felt comfortable around women. He had had a few girlfriends over the years, but none had lasted. Now, here, he was face to face, with probably the most beautiful woman he had ever seen. And she was looking back. No, that couldn't be. Cabel had never figured himself as a handsome man, by any means. He had too many scars to be considered handsome. But, she was looking. *"Probably, just because I'm a stranger"* he finally concluded. After all, he had not bathed in days, outside of a creek he might find, along the way. And then, there was no soap. His clothes, mostly homemade, were dirty from days on the trail. And he was in bad need of a shave.

"Come on in, Cabel, let's eat a bite and we'll talk," Bob Sheah finally broke the trance that had taken over Cabel.

The house was like most western houses, at the time, made of log with a thatch roof, but Cabel could see the care that had been taken in the construction. The front and back door were fit perfectly into place, which was important here, due to the severely cold winters. The windows were made with the same care as the doors, tightly fit and with crosses cut in them, to allow for shooting, through with minimal danger inside. Most of the furniture had been brought with them from Atlanta and had survived the trip in amazingly good condition. All was very neat, clean, and snug inside. This would be a wonderful place to live and grow.

"Well, what's on your mind, Cabel?" Bob Sheah asked, as they sat down at the table. The smell of food was floating through the house like it was always there. And, Cabel thought, it probably was.

"I'm not sure yet. My brother Dave is coming out soon and I had hoped to have the place set up pretty much, when he got here. But I wasn't expecting all this. I need to warn him of what's going on, before he leaves, so he won't walk into a trap. And, I need to find somewhere to park some livestock, until I can get all this straight. You got any idea where I might be able to hide a couple hundred head of cows for a while?" Cabel, as of yet, had no plan of action to follow. But he knew what would have to be done and knew it would have to be done soon or the snow would block all the passes, before he could get any stock brought in. Also, he had no idea, yet, how he was going to get the stock. He had money, with which, to buy it, but no way to go get it, without leaving here. And, he didn't want to leave right now. He needed to stay here and let people know who he was, maybe build a reputation of sorts. He knew that if he left, things would be said about him, and by the time he returned, he would not be wanted around here.

Bob Sheah sat thoughtfully for a minute, as if wondering whether or not he should put this much trust in a man he had met only today. This could be another trick used by Brantley, but he really didn't believe it was.

"Yeah, over west of here, there's a hanging valley. Maybe a hundred acres or so. I think if a man looked, he would be able to find a trail big enough to bring in a herd. But, it's hard to find, and once winter settles in, it will be too late. You won't never get anything in there. Now, as far as warning your brother, the nearest Cabel is in Steamboat, southeast of here. Pretty good size town and a lot of cattle come through there, you might be able to pick up a herd there, too, talk to a man named Jack Nelson. You'll find him at the 'Last Chance Saloon'. Big fellow, wears black all the time. Tell him I sent you to him, he'll probably set you up, if not, he'll put you in touch with someone who can. But, this ain't going to be easy, son. These Brantleys have got this part of the country all sewed up. Those who aren't in with them, either think highly of them or are scared of them, so you watch yourself, boy. They'll shoot you in the back, if they feel they need to. The old man, he's not so bad, but that boy of his, is. You had better not take a step, without looking where you are going, or they'll get you."

Sarah had brought their food and they had eaten, while they talked; now, Bob Sheah pushed himself away from the table and got up.

"Well, Cabel, I've got things to do, and as you can see, we're a man short right now, so I don't have time to sit around. I'd ask you to help but you've got things to do as well. And if I were you, I'd be getting to them. But you remember what I said, watch yourself. Otherwise, you'll wind up dead in these mountains somewhere and no one will ever know what happened."

That being said, he walked out and left Cabel alone to think. He had guessed that Willow Springs would not have a wire, but now, he knew where he would have to go to send one.

He wondered, then, about Slick Montgomery. Had he quit the Brantleys? If so, how did that go? For he knew that Slick would not just ride off into the night, without saying anything, he would have to go tell the old man he was leaving.

Would he say anything about the talk that they had? Cabel decided that it was unlikely that he would. Slick knew how much trouble was going to start, when the word of the lost deed got out. And all that would happen soon enough.

Sarah had come back into the room now and was busy picking up the kitchen from the hastily thrown together meal that she had prepared.

"That was sure a fine meal, ma'am, I appreciate it," Cabel tossed off the last drops of his coffee and rising, he put on his hat.

"You'll be leaving us, then?" she asked.

"Yes, ma'am. I've got a lot of things to tend to and not much time to tend to them."

"Yes, I'm sorry but couldn't help but to overhear some of your conversation. Sounds like you've bit off a chunk."

"Yes, ma'am, that it does. But, sometimes, that's what happens. Now, I've got to figure out how to chew it up without choking," Cabel chuckled at the play on words. He had always enjoyed that.

"If you had time to wait a day or two, I could have Sandy show you where that valley is. He's only been here a few years, but, already, knows every inch of this country. He's told me about that valley, says he wants to build him a house up there someday."

"Sandy? That wouldn't be Sandy Pearson, would it?"

"Why, yes. Yes, it is. Do you know him?"

"Yes, ma'am, I do. Haven't seen him in a couple years though. We punched cows together, some back in Arkansas. There's a good man right there, Mrs. Sheah. He's here working for you, then?"

"Yes and you're right, he is a good man."

"It'll be good to see Sandy again, but right now, I've got to go. Tell him I'm here for me, would you, ma'am. I'll be back in a few days, if that's okay."

With that, Cabel walked out of the house and into the afternoon sun. He had a lot to do and there was no use in waiting any longer to get started. First thing he would do, would be to go into town and check things out. Maybe, then, he would head out to Steamboat and get a message off to Dave. He would be leaving soon, but they had agreed, ahead of time, that Dave would stop, when he could and check the wire offices for a message, just in case something were to happen.

Mounting his horse, he rode out of the yard and down the trail toward town. Then, as an afterthought, he left the trail and moved over next to the trees where he would not be as easily seen.

Chapter Six

The lights were still on in the house, when Slick Montgomery rode into the yard at the five-b ranch, belonging to Cobb Brantley. His decision to leave the ranch would not be looked upon with any favor. He knew how Cobb was and Cobb did not like to lose employees, especially those who were known to be good with a gun. But things had gone out of control lately and Slick was not the kind of man to do the things, which he knew he would be asked to do, eventually.

The sound of Tough's voice broke through his thoughts from the lighted bunkhouse.

"Took you long enough."

The contempt in the young man's voice was obvious. Even in the dark, Slick could picture Tough standing there, rifle in hand, glaring up at him, on his horse.

"I ain't in no hurry, Tough. You, now, on the other hand, you must be in a hurry for something. Sneaking up on a man in the dark like that," Slick had stopped his horse and pulled out the makings of a smoke.

"What do you mean by that?"

"Don't you know in all of your infinite wisdom that that's a good way to get yourself killed? I've never liked you anyway, Tough, I might've just turned and shot at the voice. Had I been an edgy man."

"Where you been, anyway?"

"None of your business, Tough. I don't work for you."

"Is that a fact? Well, just give it time. The old man has already said he's going to leave all this to me," he made a wide gesture with his hand, as if to take in the whole valley, "Then, we'll see who works for who, won't we, Slick."

"Yea, kid, I guess we will. Is the old man up?"

"Yea, he's up. He's been waiting for you."

"Well, sir, if you're through with me, I'll go talk to him a minute."

"Yea, sure, I'm through with you, for now. Watch your back though, Slick, 'cause I sure will be."

The two men separated there; each hating the other a little more than they did before. Each knowing what was going to happen, eventually. And each dreading to find out the outcome. For, both were fast.

The old man was seated at the table, when Slick entered the room. A tall, sinister looking man, wearing his normal black clothes. His black hat had been removed, revealing his silver hair. In his eyes was the same contempt that could easily be seen in his son's eyes; only this was born from years of trying and failing. Cobb hated anyone with the ability to succeed. Not even realizing that given the effort in the right place, he, too, would have been a success. Or if he did realize, he knew it was too late, now, to go about everything the right way.

"Howdy, Cobb," Slick's nerves were all on end now; for he knew that the old man had to know what was about to happen.

"Tell me about this character ya'll met in the valley."

"Not much to tell really, just a drifting cowboy. Knew him a few years ago in Missouri, good kid, just a little rambunctious sometimes."

"He looking for work?" The old man knew what was going to happen and what he was going to have to do about it, but he liked Slick, so he was giving him every option out he could think of.

"No, says he's looking for a place to settle down. You know, same ol' story, tired of drifting."

"Got any place in particular in mind?"

Well, here it was, he had been wondering, if he would be able to lie to the old man or not. He knew full well if the word of the deed got out, it would mean the end of peace in this valley, but it was going to get out soon enough anyway, might as well let the boy do it in his own time.

"No, not right now, just looking. Said he figures there is enough room in this valley for everyone, if they want to get along," Slick was hoping for the best in the old man to come out, but at the same time, he knew better.

"Tough says he figures you're getting ready to quit. Is he right?"

Just realizing he was tired already and that this was going to be a long night, Slick got up and poured himself a cup of coffee from the wood stove. Then, as he walked back to the table with the coffee in his left hand, he replied,

"You know me, Cobb, I used to be a good lawman. And I still believe in the law. Now, it's none of my business what you do, but I've a feeling things are getting ready to get real ugly around here."

"Yea, you used to be a lawman, but all that went downhill, when you killed that kid in Tucson. Now, you're just like me and the rest of these boys here, riding the outlaw trail, with gun in hand, and watching your back trail to make sure nobody follows you. Now, you're going to tell what you know about this kid, then you and me, we are going to work this out. Nobody quits me, Slick, and you, least of all. Not after all I've done for you."

"Yea, Cobb, I'm quitting, and there ain't a damn thing you can do about it. Now, I'm going to ease on out of here and you're going to sit here nice and quiet like, while I do. I'm not asking for any trouble here; all I want to do is go about my way in peace. But you know me, Cobb; if you want trouble, you'll damn well have it. And as for that kid in Tucson, that was an accident and you know it."

"You can tell that to the law, when they find you. You killed the mayor's son, boy, you'll hang and you know it."

"Maybe, but it won't be for anything you talked me into."

His right hand held his revolver now, as he set down his cup and backed his way to the door.

"Be seeing you, Cobb."

"You know I'll kill you now, don't you, Slick?"

Slick didn't answer. Once out the front door he made his way through the shadows to his horse. Once mounted, he left nothing more than a cloud of dust in his wake. The lights in the bunkhouse were still on and he could hear the men, as they went about their card game, but there was no way out of the ranch yard that could not be watched and he knew that Tough would be watching. So, he ran his horse hard, until he cleared the immediate area of the ranch, then turning sharply to the left, he headed for the trees. Once in the trees, he was able to slow down and walk his horse. He needed to see if anyone had followed him from the ranch. Once satisfied he was not followed, he pointed his mount toward town. He knew there was going to be trouble and he needed to find Cabel to warn him.

He knew that Cabel would still be in his camp, but there was no use riding there tonight. It would take him the rest of the night to get there, and then would be left with no rest at all, should something happen. No, it would be better to simply go to town and meet up with him there, where some of the suspicion would be clouded by the chance that they had ran into each other. If Cabel was going to pull this off, it would take some serious planning, on both of their parts.

Still figuring he had been followed, he made a cold camp. He didn't have many supplies with him anyway, so he rolled in his blankets and tried to rest. His horse, he had left saddled, in case of trouble.

For a long time, he lay awake, listening to the sounds of the night. He could hear his horse crunching grass as, he ate and somewhere not far-off, a coyote howled. His horse, as were a lot of them in those days, had been recently captured from the wild. Slick knew that because of this as he would get some warning before anyone could get near him. His horse would get spooked and whinny, if he heard anything out of the ordinary, for wild horses knew what dangers the night could hold.

He slept, but fitfully. Since that night in Tucson, he had been plagued with dreams, always ending with the look in the young man's eyes, as he died. Looking at him, accusing him, always asking why.

He had no idea if there was a warrant out for him or not. He had taken off more out of his own guilt than of any the town may have put on him. He had not meant to kill the boy; of course, he had simply been in the wrong place at the wrong time. Had Slick known the boy was even close, he would never have pulled the trigger. But what's done cannot be undone, so he had taken off. And next thing he knew, he was, in danger of becoming a real outlaw, under the direction of Cobb Brantley.

But that was yesterday, now, maybe, he would have the chance to regain some of the self-respect he had lost only a few years ago in Tucson. If only he could help, this young man get what was rightfully his and bring the others to some form of justice.

He was up before the sun and on his way. He had only ridden a few miles in the dark. His first thought had been to keep going, but he knew that that's what would be expected of him. Also, he had been tired and a tired man doesn't think as well as he should sometimes.

Now, he had to get to Willow Springs and find Cabel. He had no idea whether he would be there now or not, but he would have to get a message to him. And he knew he needed to get out of town for a while. It would help matters, if the Brantleys thought he had left after quitting. Maybe, he would be able to take some of the pressure off of Cabel. For once, they knew they were working together, they would know that something was up, for sure. And once word got out it, was going to get bad around Willow Springs.

He was only ten miles from town, when he realized he was falling from his horse. He hadn't realized he was shot, until moments later, when he heard the sharp report of the rifle. Then, the pain hit him. *"It's funny,"* he thought, *"How, sometimes, you have to know you're hurt before you feel the pain. Like when you cut yourself working and don't know until someone asks what happened."*

Slick could feel his mind slipping into a place he dared not go, for if he did, the Brantleys would surely find him and finish him off. He had to move, to take cover, to stay awake, and to stay alive.

The bullet had been fired from behind him and had hit him in the lower right side. Although it had passed all the way through, it had taken a good chunk of meat with it. Slick didn't think anything vital had been hit; however, he was losing a lot of blood and fast.

He forced himself up to his knees and as quickly as he could, he made his way into the brush beside the trail. His horse had not run off but was out of reach for the time being and with it, all of his supplies. Thinking quickly, he tore a piece off of his shirttail to put in the hole left by the bullet. The pain was excruciating but he had no choice, if he didn't stop the bleeding or at least slow it, he would surely die. And this was not the way he had figured on going out. He had too many things to do. His name to clear. And, now, a debt to pay to Cobb Brantley. He must get through this. First things first, he had to get to his horse. His pistols had stayed in their holsters, thanks to the thongs he had to hold them in, however, his rifle was still in the rifle boot on his saddle. He would have to have that, if he was to survive. Also, on his horse, were his pack, with the few medical supplies he carried and his water. He was only ten miles or so from town and a doctor, and he had to make it. There would be no help coming from anywhere, so he would have to do it alone.

He knew the Brantleys would be watching for him to come out in the open, so he must stay hidden from sight, as much as possible. Right now, he was sure they knew he was still alive, so they would not come down after him. But he knew they would take another shot at him, if he allowed one, so every step must be with caution. If only he knew where the shot had come from exactly, it would help matters considerably. So, without moving any more than necessary, he surveyed the country around where he thought the shot may have come from.

From where he sat, he could see nothing more than trees and rocks, but there had to be something, somewhere. It would be above him, of that, he was sure, and it would have to be somewhere the shooter could get, out of easily, without being seen. Looking over the surrounding area again, something caught his eye, like a reflection of light, off of a rifle barrel. But it was in the wrong spot. The shot could not have come from there. So, the shooter or shooters, for there, were probably more than one was moving. Trying to get around and cut him off. If they were successful, it would be over for him. He must move now. He must get to his horse and mount him somehow, before the shooters could gain a new advantage.

Managing, with the help of a tree trunk, he got to his feet and started moving in the direction his horse would have went. He had heard of people who could just whistle, and their horse would come running, but he didn't believe it. Not in this country, anyway. The horses here, or most of them, were fresh off of the range and still part wild. And given the opportunity, they would be wild again. He had heard of wild horses being captured with pieces of saddle still clinging to their back. But he knew his horse and took care of it. He knew that it would not run off...yet. It would be nice though, if all he had to do was whistle. He was going to have to learn that trick.

Staying as far out in the brush as he could and still see the trail, he worked his way along, pausing from time to time to look around and rest. His strength was starting to fail him, now, from the loss of blood but he had no choice, he had to move. If the shooters got in front of him, he would be cut off and would, without any doubt, die out here.

Sitting and listening, he could hear a stream, not far-off, running down the side of the mountain, gurgling and sipping, as it made its way down to the valley below. Wait, sipping, there was something drinking out of the stream. Knowing that all animals, when in doubt, go to water, he knew, at once, it was his horse, that beautiful line back Dunn that had carried him so many miles in these last few months. Easing his way through the trees, he moved in the direction of the sound, until, finally, he rounded a mound of rocks and saw him standing there, just as he had pictured drinking from the stream, about fifty yards away. Out in the open.

Slick swore softly to himself and again wished for that whistle trick. But it was not going to work. He would have to get across the open spot very quickly, which, in his condition, was no small feat, but, also, without spooking the horse. He could circle around some and get a few yards closer. Suddenly the horse's head came up. Had he smelled something? Maybe, it was Slick himself or the blood he had smelled. Either way, he had smelled something and was about to spook.

"Easy boy. Its' just me," he spoke, hopefully, only loud enough for the horse to hear.

Almost at the same instant, he spoke he heard voices. Two men headed this way looking for something. They had gotten in front of him, then. It was not going to be easy from here on out, unless he could get to his horse and make a run for it. He could not make out their words, only he did recognize their voices; the Lawton boys. *"What a shame,"* he thought. These boys had it in them to be good men, only they had been corrupted by the Brantleys. Slick had tried to talk to the boys several times, to give them some guidance to the right path, but they idolized Tough and Cobb Brantley. Now, here they were, hunting down the one person who had tried to teach them to do what they knew was the right thing. And if they found him, he would have to kill them. Or be killed himself.

From the sound of the voices, the boys were coming from his right and below him, on the mountain. So, that meant there were at least three, probably, four men, up there, looking for him. But he knew vaguely where all were located and that was a plus. If he could get on his horse, he may just get out.

Talking ever so quietly to keep his horse calm, he made his way around to the closest point he could find, then in one extremely painful leap, he was aboard. He had thought, at first, he wouldn't make it and if his horse had spooked at all, he wouldn't have. Only the talking had kept the horse calm and still. But, now, he was riding again, with his rifle in his hand. He was going to make it.

He took the nearest game trail he could find, going in the right direction and hit it at a dead run. He might've been able to sneak away, but they were just too close.

Bullets ricocheted off of the trees, as he ran. His attackers were on foot, so he knew that soon, he would be out of reach. If he could make it out of the trees and into the flat land of the valley, he would be clear. So, he kept going, ignoring the harsh breath sounds of his horse, knowing that if his horse died, so would he, but, at this point, he had no choice.

Leaving the trees, he entered the valley at this pace, he wasn't far away from Willow Springs and safety. At least, for now. But he could feel his strength fading fast and began to wonder again, if he would make it. But he had to. There was no choice in the matter. He had to get to town and let Cabel know what was happening. He had to get to the Doctor in town and get treated, before the infection set in. He had not even had time, yet, to wash his wound out with water, now his shirttail that had been stuffed in the hole was soaked with blood, and the movements he had had to endure were not helping. He needed to get somewhere safe; where he would be able to lie down and rest, so the bleeding would stop.

Topping a low rise, he could see the town spread out before him. He was still a couple miles away, but just the sight of town made Slick feel better about his chances. He had lost any pursuit for the time being, so was able to slow his horse to walk and catch his breath. His wounded side was bleeding bad now and he had been hit in the thigh by a ricochet, when running through the trees. The second wound was not that bad, although it was very painful and added to the blood loss from his side.

The whole world seemed to spin. He looked up at the sun, high in the sky now, and judged it to be around noon. It was getting hot now and the heat did nothing to make him feel better. One false move now and this close or not, his chances weren't good. He could feel himself slipping from the saddle little by little, trying with all his might to stay erect, as best as he could.

Descending the last rise, he entered Willow Springs. Its dusty streets were a welcome sight to a man in his condition. He could see Doc Bush's office, ahead on the right but something was wrong. He was falling, no, he was being pulled, from the saddle by someone. His last memories were of a woman with blue eyes and blonde hair. No idea who it belonged to, but it gave him something else to dream of, which was a welcome change.

Chapter Seven

Once leaving the ranch, Cabel had time to take stock and sort out the last few days. The Brantleys wished to control everything but, actually, had no right to anything. Why were they so intent upon having the old Williams place, anyway? There was land everywhere, just for the taking. All a man had to do was find some land that no one else had already claimed and file on it. What was so special about this place that made Cobb Brantley just have to have it? He would have to get out there and have a look around, eventually, but for the time being, it didn't matter. That land belonged to Dave and Cabel Glaize and they would have it.

His thoughts shifted to Slick Montgomery, where did he stand in all this? They had made an agreement at the camp last night, but how loyal was the man to Cobb Brantley? Did he quit last night, or had he decided against it? Would he tell the Brantleys about the deed that he and Dave possessed? Or would he be true to his word and be waiting on him, right now, in town?

And then there were the Sheahs. They were definitely a capable bunch, but would they truly fight. They had fought when attacked by the Brantleys, but that was different. They had been left no choice. Bob had seemed to Cabel like the kind of man who would rather let well enough alone than to push the issue, but time would tell. He wished, though, that he hadn't said anything to Bob Sheah about the deed. But would Bob have accepted him the same? Cabel doubted it.

The fewer people that knew about the deed, the better off he was. Of course, he did not have it himself; Dave would be bringing it out with him. But, if possible, he needed to let people think he had it, those who knew about it, anyway, in order to take the pressure off of Dave, when he did come out. He would be glad to see Dave. He needed someone out here he knew he could trust. But Dave wouldn't even have left yet, and then, it was at least another little while, before he would arrive. So, he was on his own for another two weeks or so. That would be plenty of time to have the place set up, without the current troubles, but it didn't look good for staying in their own cabin this winter. They would have to make-due with what they could.

What about that hanging valley that Sheah had talked about? If he could get a herd of cows up there, that would be a good place to last out the winter. Cabel knew, then, that he must get up there and scope it out. Mrs. Sheah had said that Sandy was interested in settling it in the future. Why hadn't he filed on it already? What was the hold up, Sandy had never been one to fool around, when the time came to act, so what was his problem now?

Cabel scoped the country out, on his way to Willow Springs. It was a beautiful land. Not much grass in places, but most of it was good land and would have no problem supporting a good-sized herd. There was water, almost everywhere you looked. He wished he knew what his place looked like. He had a mental picture of it, of course, but wanted to see it for himself. Williams had told them of grass and water, but did Williams know what it would take to raise a herd of cows? What if the place weren't worth fooling with? What then? Then, this fight was going to be useless. But, had that been true, then Cobb Brantley would not be trying so hard to keep it. Also, Slick would've said something. No, it was a good place. No doubt about that. But was there something else that made Brantley want it? In time, Cabel would be able to get out and have a good look around. But, for the time being, he had other things that would have to be done.

Cabel had no clear plan to follow right now, he had a lot of things he needed to do but, as of yet, had no clue where to start. He had always had a habit of letting the chips fall where they may and, at least so far, they had fallen in his direction. However, this was different. There was too much on the line. Too much to lose. And not just for himself, but for his older brother, Dave, as well. The two of them had each poured in their life savings on this deal and, now, it was up to Cabel to protect it. It was a new position for Cabel to be in and it wasn't a favorable one. He had always felt, as if he played with a stacked deck because it's easy to win, when there's nothing to lose. But, now, he had everything to lose. His approach would have to be different.

As the road turned to the south, he entered the town of Willow Springs. It wasn't much, but, then, neither were most western towns. Someone would be traveling and either break down or sometimes just get tired of moving. Most time, it was next to a major source of water, such as this one, other times, it was the scenery. But no matter what the reason, someone would stop. Then, someone else. Next thing was a store, then maybe a saloon. Eventually a town would grow from where there was nothing a few years or sometimes, even months earlier. Some would last for lifetimes, some only a short period. Others, not at all.

This town was probably no more than a couple years old. The dusty streets were those of every other town of the era. The buildings all of wood frame, already starting to fade from the effects of the weather. But this one was different, for even though no one here knew him yet, this was his town. This was where he would make his home. The general store was where he would buy his supplies. And the doctor's office where his children would visit when hurt or sick. Ahead on the left, was the Dipsy Doodle Saloon. Cabel had given up drinking, but the saloons in the west were not just drinking places, they were meeting places. Places to go, when information was needed or needed to be shared.

Cabel Glaize rode his horse up to the hitch rail and dismounted. How many times in the future would he do this? Would he ever actually get to fulfill this dream that had gone so awry in just the few short days, since he arrived here? His first time in town and already, he had to wonder who was here waiting for him or what had been said about this newcomer, who just arrived but planned to stay.

Inside, the room was cool and surprisingly well-kept. The floors had been freshly cleaned in anticipation of the crowd that would gather there tonight. The room was bigger than he had originally guessed; being deeper than it was wide. There were three poker tables in one corner, off to the left and a piano in the other corner, opposite. Against the back wall, was a stage of sorts for an entertainer to stand and the rest of the room was filled with tables for eating or just sitting and drinking. The dance floor would have to be made from moving the tables, whenever one was needed.

The bar was on the left wall and extended through most of the building. Made of solid oak, it would have to have been brought in special, which meant this owner had no intention of leaving any time soon. Walking up to the bar, the bartender appeared from behind the curtain that led into the back room and probably, the office.

"Whiskey?" the bartender asked. He was like most bartenders in the west, tough and capable, with dark eyes showing from under his thick black hair and beard. He wore overalls now but Cabel knew these were only worn during the day, when there was no one to dress up for. Tonight, he would be dressed up to look the part of a businessman. Another type of person would not have been able to stay in business long with the type of people he served. In the larger towns, this was not a problem due to the availability of law enforcement; however, out on the frontier, that was not usually the case. Someone was always subject to get out of hand and it would be the barkeeps job to protect his establishment.

"No, thank you. Coffee's good for me, unless you've got some grub cooked up, back there, somewhere."

"I think there's some beans and a biscuit or two left from lunch, I'll be back."

As the barkeep left, Cabel glanced at his pocket watch, the only thing he had left from his father, after the fire had killed his parents. Six o'clock, the place would soon be filling up with the usual crowd of miners and cowboys. There would be lots of drinking and probably, some fighting, but there would be some business conducted here, too. Maybe, not tonight, but in the past and future, for these, were the places where deals were made and money changed hands.

"Heard there was a stranger around," the bartender remarked to Cabel, as he sat the food and coffee down on the bar.

"Word travels fast around here, doesn't it?"

"Not a good idea to go around bucking the Brantleys. One feller that done that is at Doc Bush' office right now. Been shot twice. Doc says he don't know yet, if'n he'll make it."

"You don't sound much like you care for the Brantleys."

"Mister, I got no dog in this fight. And the Brantleys ain't done nothing to me. As long as they want to spend money in here, that's fine by me, but if you want to get right down to it, then no, I don't guess I do."

"You aren't scared of them, like everyone else?"

"No, this is the only drinking hole for miles, and none of them have the gumption to run it. So, if something were to happen to me, it would be closed down and they know it. And, as for everyone else, they're not scared, just too blind to see what's going on around them."

"Well, I guess we got something in common already. My names Cabel Glaize."

He held out to shake hands.

"Jake Smith, nice to know you. You ain't asked about that fellow in the Docs office," Jake stated, with a knowing look in his eye.

"Should I?"

"Well, word has it, you two are friends, of a sort. Fellow named Slick Montgomery. Shot up pretty good from what I hear."

Cabel made no motion to show that he even recognized the name. But how did this man know so much already. He and Slick had only met the night before, and he himself wasn't, yet, sure of the partnership. But, he needed to get over and see Slick and see how bad he was. Slick was the only help he would have around here, until Dave made it out. But if the Brantleys were already trying to kill him, he needed to get him out of here, as soon as possible.

"Oh yeah, who'd you hear that from?"

"Tough Brantley. He was in here, earlier. And just to let you know, he says it was you who done the shooting."

"Me? Now, ain't that a kick in the pants?" Cabel tried not to let the disappointment show in his voice, as he laughed at the absurdity of the statement. He was here, trying to better himself. Trying to be more than just a saddle bum or gun hand, but not matter where he turned, he found only trouble.

"Any idea how bad off he is?" Cabel asked after a moment of thought.

"No. Not yet. Last I heard was that Kimberly Williams pulled slick from his horse and called the doc, but he had lost a sight of blood already. Looked bad, too, from what they say. Folks around thought he was already half dead."

"Kimberly Williams," Cabel thought to himself, *"Who was she? Was she kin to the same Williams, who had sold the place to him and his brother? If so, why did she not go back to Richmond with her family? And, if she stayed, why did she not own the ranch now? Wouldn't the obvious thing to do be to leave the ranch to someone who was going to stay, anyway?"*

Cabel knew he had some figuring to do now. It seemed, as if, Williams had sold them a bundle of grief, more than a ranch. This was turning into a nightmare. He had known things, such as this, to go on for years. But it wouldn't be years this time. He and Dave had worked hard to save what little money they had and no two-bit outlaw would keep them from their dream.

Cabel paid the barkeep and got up, "Is there a marshal in town?"

"Yeah, but he won't be in his office right now. You go on about your business, then come back later. He'll be in, from time to time, tonight. I'll tell him you're looking for him."

"Alright, thanks… Does he already know Tough is blaming this on me?" Cabel asked as an afterthought.

"If I know Tough, then yeah he told him. But you don't worry too much, at least, not unless Slick dies. If he lives, he'll know who shot him. But I'd still watch my backside, if I were you. You know how these small-town marshals can be…"

"Yeah, I hear you... Thanks for the advice."

It was dark out now and walking out of the room, Cabel could see lights shining through the windows of the businesses and homes. Soon, he would know all of these people. Some he would call friend, some he would only be acquainted with, but he would know all of them.

He paused at the doorway to let his eyes adjust to the light and have a look around, before stepping out into the street. He was, or soon would be, a wanted man. He had no intention of running, for he was innocent. He would go to the marshal and tell him his side of the story, it was that simple. He had been with the Sheahs all day; there was no way he could have done the shooting. That was, if the marshal would go talk to them.

His eyes were working, as well as his mind. He searched every shadow and every doorway, looking for anything out of place. Nothing seemed out of the ordinary, but something wasn't right. He had the feeling of being watched or hunted, but nothing was there. A dog crossed the dusty road, headed toward the rear of the saloon, probably looking for scraps. A horse stamped restlessly at the hitching rail to his left.

Suddenly, the dog, which had been so intent on entering the alley between the buildings, turned left and headed up the boardwalk away from him. What had turned him? Had he seen something there to change his mind? Not taking any chances, Cabel moved suddenly to his left, and staying close to the wall, so as not to leave the shadows, made his way down the walk and around the corner into an alley that ran between the saloon and the general store. There, he stopped, hiding behind some barrels and waited. In the shadows as he was, no one would be able to see him, unless they were right up close, which was what Cabel was hoping for. He wanted to see if anyone came out looking for him.

He was there only a minute before he began to hear footsteps on the walk and then a figure lurked before him, nothing recognizable, only a silhouette being cast from the light on the other side of the street. The man was obviously looking for someone and since no one else had come this way, Cabel knew who this man looked for.

"Looking for me?" Cabel had waited for the man to turn his head away, before stepping out from his hiding spot. He had stepped out suddenly, in order to hopefully startle the man and throw him off guard and it had worked. Drawing his pistol as he walked out, he spoke again to the startled man, "Who are you and what do you want with me?"

"It ain't me who wants anything with you, boy, but a man who does paid me a good price to give you a message."

"Let me guess…Brantley? So, what's the message? I don't have all night."

The man was no longer startled, if he truly had been at all. He, now, stood facing Cabel with a sinister grin on his face that told all the confidence this man had in his ability, "If you'll let me drop this gun belt, I'll give it to you just like I was paid to do."

Cabel had seen this before. He, like his brother, had tried his hand at prize fighting, but, for some reason, his heart wasn't in it. He liked the fighting part; it was just that it took all the fun out of it, when you were being paid.

However, he had done more than his share of fighting in the saloons and cow camps all over the country, before he went back home a few months ago, "Look, whoever you are, I don't have the time to spend putting knots all over your heard. So, if you've got something you want to say, say it and be done. I plan on spending the rest of my life, right here, in this little town; we'll have plenty of chances to go at it later. Right now, I've got business to tend to."

"No, I was paid to do a job and I plan on earning my money," the man was smiling now; his over-confidence glowing so bright, Cabel could see it though the darkness, "Now, unless you're yellow, drop that shooter and let's get down to business."

"Alright, I'll oblige but make no mistake, you'll be the one receiving the message and I'm gonna do it right, so all your friends can understand that this ain't no tender-foot they're messing with. You want a beating, you got it," Cabel said, as he removed his gun belt and laid it on the barrel next to him.

The pleasure on the man's face was obvious; he had never been beaten and knew that it couldn't happen. No one around here was man enough to whip Lucky Parnell, let alone this drifting young cowhand.

As Cabel set down his belt, he talked to the man, "Who are you, anyway? I've never liked beating a man what I didn't know his name."

"Lucky Parnell, but ain't no need in worrying about that. I've never been beaten."

"Lucky, huh?" Cabel said with a chuckle, as he hooked his toe in the dirt and sent it flying into the eyes of his adversary. Cabel followed the dirt all the way in and struck first with an overhand right that started the blood to flow over Lucky's left eyebrow.

The big man was staggered, but this was nothing new to him. He had fought all of his life. It was his way and this meant he had finally found someone who might put up a fight for a few minutes.

Cabel had backed off now, to let the bigger man get his bearing. Beating this man wasn't enough; he had to do it right. He had to send everyone the message that he not only would stand his ground but was also capable of it.

He stared at the bigger man now, as he waited, thinking how many times had this man fought, without even considering that he could be whipped. What kind of past did this man have that gave him such confidence? It really didn't matter at this point; Cabel intended to beat this man soundly, if for no other reason than to let his enemies know he would not be pushed.

The big man had regained himself now and hunkered down opposite Cabel, who had gone into a boxer's stance. They circled each other warily, until Cabel's back was to the street, then the big man lunged. Cabel side-stepped the lunge and with a shove, sent the bigger man head first into the dusty street and again, waited for the man to rise.

This time Lucky was more cautious. Perhaps, he was starting to wonder if he had done the right thing by taking Brantley's money. He was still thinking about this as Cabel moved in, jabbing with his left that struck twice, before Lucky was able to parry, then came again with his overhand right that struck again in the same place as before. Now, Lucky was wary. The confident smile on his face had been replaced with an expression of anger. Again, he lunged trying to get hold of Cabel, so he could use his superior strength and this time, he was successful. Cabel tried to sidestep again, but this time the big man was ready for him and caught him in his left arm and sent both men to the ground. Cabel knew if he allowed this man to use his strength, he wasn't going to last long and his fears were proven warranted as the big man struck, lights flashed in Cabel's head over and over again, as Lucky went to work. Forcing himself to roll cover, Cabel was able to rise to his hands and knees and finally, get back to his feet. Turning around, he hooked his toe behind the bigger man's foot and shoved. The bigger man went to the ground but not before grabbing Cabel's shirt and taking him down with him. But, this time Cabel was on top and it was his turn to go to work. Lucky was still punching at him from his back; however, he couldn't draw back, so there was no real power behind them and so Cabel was able to throw right and left at the man's unprotected face, until the bigger man finally forced the two of them, back to their feet. Now, Cabel was able to move and after throwing a few quick jabs, he went to work on the man's body. Hooking two rights into his ribs and upper cutting a left to his wind, he felt the big man starting to fail. Hooking two more rights into his ribs, he moved back up to Lucky's face. After a right hook to the cut over his eye, Cabel sent a bone crushing left hook to his jaw. Now, the man was beaten; there was no doubt. Along with the crooked way he was standing, probably due to a couple of broken ribs, there was blood flowing freely down the man's face and his jaw was hanging in a funny, distorted way.

"Earn your money yet?" Cabel asked, as he stepped back to give the man some room.

"Alright, Mr. Brantley says he wants you out of town by tomorrow night or he'll come hunting you himself. And by the way, you're right, we'll get another turn at this."

"Well, Lucky, you go back and tell Brantley if he ain't man enough to tell me himself the first time, then I ain't going to worry too much about his idle threats. If he wants me out of town, then he can run me out. Until then, stay out of my way. He'll know soon enough what my business is here, because I'll tell him, when I'm ready. Now, you go tell him that and when this is all over, if you've healed up and feeling cocky, we'll try this again."

With that being said, Cabel brushed past Lucky and made his way across the street to the doc's office where, luckily, lights were still shining through the windows. It wasn't until he turned and looked back across the street from the doctor's office that he realized a crowd had gathered in front of the saloon, wanting to find out what the commotion was. He could hear the whispers and feel the stares, as he continued on his way. Now, the crowd was dispersing and the laughter and gayety of the evening could begin.

As he reached the doctor's office, a soft rap on the door brought an immediate response from inside.

"Who is it?" a woman's voice answered.

"A friend, I come to check on Slick. May name is Cabel Glaize."

"Go away. Come back tomorrow. It's too late tonight," the voice answered.

"I just wanted to see how he's doing and..." he decided it was worth the chance, "I need to talk to you. It's about your uncle."

"How do you know who I am?"

"Aren't you Kimberly Williams, Niece to August Williams?"

"How do you know my uncle or me for that matter? I've never even heard of you, except..."

"Except for what?" Cabel, now, knew that this girl knew who she was talking to. Either Slick had said something, or she had been in contact with August Williams, the man, who had sold the deed to he and his brother, "Let me in so we can talk."

Cabel heard the bolt being removed from the door and, in an instant, it was opened into the outer room of the doctor's office. Although the room was only faintly lit, Cabel could see well enough to make out the bare contents of the room and the features of the figure before him.

The room was bare, except for a desk and file cabinet where Cabel knew all the medical records would be kept and a bookshelf, along the right wall. This building, as others he had seen in town, was put together well and with the care of someone who enjoyed their work. It was likely the same man who had built most of these buildings.

The woman, who stood in front of him, was a remarkable beautiful woman. She had blonde hair and big round eyes. Cabel could not tell the color in this light; however, he could make out most of her other features. She was tall and proud, with a figure that would match against any woman Cabel had ever seen. She looked at him now with a puzzled look on her face, undoubtedly due to the mention of her uncle's name.

"How is he?" Cabel asked, after taking in his surroundings briefly.

"He is doing better. His fever has broken. The doctor has stopped all of the bleeding. I think he will make it, now. How do you know who I am?"

"Wild guess, more than anything. I knew your uncle in Virginia. The bartender told me your name and after some figuring, I knew you couldn't be his daughter, so you would have to be his niece, if you were kin at all."

"But there are Williams all over that aren't kin. How did you know we were kin at all?"

"Didn't, for sure, but what are the chances of two Williams families in the area? And, besides, I had to figure a way in here. I didn't figure you would just let me in here to see a man, who had just been shot. Without knowing who had done the shooting. I'm sorry if I've upset or offended you in any way," he replied honestly.

The two sat quietly for a moment, before Cabel went on with his story, "I know your uncle from Virginia. He had some business with my brother and I and that's what brings me here to Willow Springs."

Then, after a minute of thought, Cabel asked, "You said that you had never heard of me except… What did you mean by that?"

"When Slick first came in, he was delirious. He kept saying your name, but no one had ever heard of you. We didn't know who he was talking about. He acted, as if we should tell you what had happened, but no one knew how to contact you. Some thought he was saying that you were the one who had shot him and then, Tough came into the saloon and blamed it on you and that, of course, made everything worse."

"Well, I didn't shoot him. We are going into a partnership. He was supposed to quit the Brantleys last night, then meet me here in town. They must have followed him, when he left the ranch and tried to dry gulch him, before he could get back to town."

Looking around, Cabel found a pencil and some paper lying on the desk. Picking them up, he looked back up to Kimberly, "When he wakes up, would you give him a note for me?"

"Sure. He should be waking up before long. He's a strong man."

With that, Cabel wrote a note and after folding it, gave it to Kimberly, "Tell him I had to leave for a few days to contact my brother and will be back in a week or two. Tell him to meet at this place, when I get back. Right now, I have to see if I can find the town marshal and explain what's up, before he comes looking for me. It was nice to meet you."

That being said, Cabel started for the door.

"Wait, Mr. Glaize, what about my uncle? Is he still alive?"

"Yes, at least, he was, last I seen him. He was doing quite well for himself actually."

The last was a lie, for when they had met the man, he was down to his last dollar or else, he wouldn't have sold the ranch to them as cheap as he did. But, he had plans for the money that should be paying off by now, so, maybe, he wasn't lying after all. Either way, Cabel knew that, more than likely, Kimberly would never see her uncle again, so there was no need in causing her to worry over him, "We'll talk more at another time. Right now, I have to go. Please give this note to Slick and tell him what I am doing, when he wakes up."

Outside, Cabel could hear the tinkling of the piano and the roar of laughter from the saloon that was going full bore now. He had spent more time at the doctor's office than he had planned, but he had planned to spend the night in town, anyway. As he crossed the dusty street to his horse, he noticed the lights were still on at the livery, so, once he retrieved the dun, he headed to the livery stable to see about a stall for the night.

A young man of no more than twelve years opened the door, before Cabel had even arrived at the stable.

"Heard you coming up the road, mister. Figured not to make you wait," he said as he took the reins from Cabel's hand.

"This your place, son? Where's your pa?"

"He's over at the Doodle, getting drunk again, I reckon. He's done a lot of that, since Ma died last year," he said, as he put Cabel's horse in a stall and started removing the gear, "It'll be two bits for the stall and for another dime, I'll rub him down good and grain him. He sure looks like he could use it."

"That he could, boy. You just give him what you think he needs and if there is anymore I owe you, we'll square up in the morning. How does that sound?" Cabel asked, as he handed the young man the money.

"Works for me, mister, but if you are who I think you are, you had better be watchin' your back. There are several men in town looking for you, least of all, is the marshal."

"Yeah, I figured as much. Thanks for the information, son. I'll see you in the morning, bright and early."

As Cabel left, the young man had already given the horse a bait of grain and was working on him, now, with a brush. Sticking his head back in the door, he said, "Don't you spoil him too bad now; I'll have a heck of a time making him leave in the morning."

The boy didn't say anything; he just turned a big smile to Cabel and then went back to his business and Cabel went back to his.

Cabel had intentions on seeing the marshal, before he left to explain his side of the story, but not he was starting to reconsider. If the marshal wanted to, he could throw in him jail and that would put a damper in his plans. He knew he would only be in there for a short time, but a short time was all he had right now. He desperately needed to get to Steamboat and get a wire off to Dave and see about the chances of getting a herd up here. He had about decided against bringing one in this year, but at least, he would learn who to talk to, and maybe, some more about what was happening, here, in Willow Springs.

Walking past the saloon, now, he could tell that the local patrons were starting to get really juiced up. Among the voices, he heard a few that he recognized. Tough and his gang were in there right now, all liquored up and ready for trouble. How he wished he was able to walk in there right now and give them all what they had coming, but too much was riding on this. He had to do this right, not because of himself, but because his brother was depending on him, also. Had this happened under different circumstances, it would all end tonight. But with things the way they were, there was nothing he could do, right now. Even, had he not decided to talk to the marshal tonight, he, now, knew that to walk into the saloon would be just like committing suicide or murder.

Passing by the saloon, he was able to glance inside. There, they were just as he had imagined, sitting at their table drinking and playing cards.

"Your day will come," he said aloud, but to himself, as he walked on by the saloon and down the street to the hotel at the far end of town.

The rooms were nice but, then, they were fairly new. The town, itself, was new on top of the fact that there were few visitors around who would require the use of a hotel. Most visitors to these sorts of towns were usually the family or guests of someone who already lived here; therefore, there was no need for a hotel. But it was nice to have one in town for the ones who had no place to stay.

Cabel knew he should leave now, while no one would be watching for him; however, he had been on the trail for months, now, and no one was keeping him for a good night's sleep. So, once he had checked the room over and closed the drapes, he slipped into the bed and was asleep almost instantly.

Chapter Eight

"One last thing Dave, before you leave, my niece, Kimberly, should still be in the area. I had to leave her with the doctor and his family, when I left because I didn't want anything to happen to her, out on the trail, on my way home. Would you please look in on her for me? Her parents died the year before I left and I had to take her into my home, but when I got ready to leave, I was scared for her. It was such a long trip. Also, she was born in Willow Springs; it is the only home she knows. I haven't seen her since I left, but she was a lovely child and by now, she would be a lovely woman. Look after her for me and write me as to how she is doing, please."

August Williams was an eastern man with western dreams. Although he had tried and failed at those dreams, they remained as much a part of his life as they were before he left home to pursue them. Now, at an age where the pursuance of those dreams would no longer be possible, he was hoping to fulfill the dreams of someone else.

Dave Glaize and his younger brother, Cabel, were as different as night and day. Yet, together, there was a family resemblance. Not as much in appearance as in spirit. Dave had been, for years now, one of the top competitors in this part of the country, while Cabel had been conquering another foe, the west. Cabel had done all the traveling that August had wanted to do in his younger years, only August didn't have the heart to go do it. His one and only attempt had failed, at least in his eyes, due to his inability to cope with the cold weather. That, in itself, was the failure that August so regretted. Now, here were two young men, who had been doing all their life, the kinds of things that august had failed at. They would be able to right his wrongs and to pick up where he had left off.

"Sure, I will, Mr. Williams. I will look her up, as soon as I get there. Anything in particular you would like me to tell her?" Dave genuinely liked this old man. They had become close friends, since the death of his parents. He had known the man for several years now but had never known August had been out west. Dave had been up and down the east coast for the last several years, as a prizefighter and having been good at it, had the opportunity to meet all the major players in several businesses. But Dave had always been drawn to this man, for some reason. Even during the last few years, when wins in the ring had been few and far between, he had always known this man was his friend.

Cabel had been away, when their parents died. It was pure chance that he had come home when he did, within days of the accident. He had been in Texas, working on a ranch, which is what he had been doing, ever since leaving home at the age of fifteen. Now, at twenty-three, Cabel had been all over the country at various times. Never had Dave known anyone, at such an early age that was as well traveled as Cabel. He had learned lessons in the last few years that could only be learned in that same circumstance. Dave had known and associated with college graduates, who were now prominent businessmen, that weren't able to keep up a conversation on the same level with Cabel. Even though Cabel was a full four years younger than he was, Dave had begun to look up to Cabel as a mentor, in some ways, in just the few days they had spent together and now, he was looking forward to a lifetime spent with his younger, but very wise brother. Working alongside of him and learning some of the lessons he had learned in the eight years that he had been away.

"Okay, you've got all the necessary paperwork you'll need to prove your ownership of the land and everything on it. I'm sorry, but the house is not all that nice, however, it will suit your needs, until you and your brother can build a new one."

"What if someone else has moved onto the place? Shouldn't it belong to them?"

"No. This deed gives you and your brother full rights to the place. Anyone, who might be living there now, is not there legally. Don't worry; your brother will know how to handle that. He'll, probably, already have all that taken care of by the time you get there. By the way, have you heard anything from him?"

"No, not since he left. He should be there by now; I reckon I'll hear something from him in a few days. I'll be checking in the various towns, along the way. I'll hear something from him soon; I'm not too worried about Cabel."

"You be careful on your way out there and let me know you made it. You're the closest family I have anymore."

Dave couldn't help but feel some apprehension, when he left his friend. Neither of them had many friends over the years and as of now, they were the only friends either of them had. But things hadn't gone the way he had hoped they would. His fighting career had come to an end, and for all the work he had put into it, he had nothing to show, except the few dollars he had used to by this ranch, along with Cabel. His mother and father had left them nothing. His father had done nothing in his life but work. He had been a hardworking man, but had never been able to get far enough ahead to put anything away for a time such as this. Now, they were gone and the only things left from their lives were he and his brother. There was nothing left here for Dave Glaize. The house had burned and although the land had been left to him, he had no money with which to rebuild, so going west was the only way.

Dave had always envied his brother for his restless spirit. A spirit they shared, only Dave had never realized it. There was a time, when he thought differently about Cabel, when he almost despised him for the same spirit, in which, he loved him for now. Cabel had left home and, therefore, left Dave to look after things, when his parents had started to age. His life had been built around his parents, in an attempt to console them for Cabel's leaving. Even though no one had any ill thoughts toward Cabel, Dave had felt the need to make up for his shortcomings. Until, finally, his father had talked to him about that subject and made him understand that Dave had his own life to live and he needed to find a way to live it. Slowly, he began to understand that the best thing he could do for his parents was to do for himself, which was about the time that his fight career began to take off. Although he could tell his mother had not liked the path he had chosen, she had always stood behind him and supported the decision. He and Cabel had always fought in one way or the other and, truthfully, Cabel had been the better fighter. He had started fighting, when he was young, before the great west had started calling but gave it up just before leaving. Dave often wondered what Cabel had thought about his decision to become a prize-fighter. If he wondered how he was doing or if he even cared; nevertheless, all that was soon to be behind him. Now, it was his turn to head for the Wild West and find out what had so attracted and held his brother all these years.

At the train station, he would begin the first leg of his journey. He was to ride the trail to Denver and then from there, it would be a stage ride to Steamboat Springs, Colorado and horseback from then on. Cabel had taken the trip on horseback the entire way, but, then, he was used to that. He had spent the biggest part of the last eight years on the back of a horse. It was where he was most comfortable. Dave on the other hand, was not. He had spent time on a horse, as had everyone, however, he had not spent enough time to get comfortable, but this would be his chance, for he really didn't have any choice.

He went straight to the Cabel office, as he had been doing daily to see if he had received any news and just like every other day, there was nothing. He had made out to not worry, when he had talked to August about this, but, in truth, he was starting to worry. Cabel had said he would let him know when he made it to Willow Springs and Cabel, if nothing else, was a man of his word. Dave should have heard something by now. But he tried not to worry, for he knew if anyone could take care of themselves, it was Cabel.

The train whistle blew twice and then Dave felt the passenger car surge forward, as the train started toward what was to be his new life, out west. He had secretly dreamed of this day for years, not knowing it would really ever happen. Yet, here it was, the start to a whole new life, a life where he could get away from 'Smoking Dave Glaize' and the fighting and just be himself.

The train left Richmond and, eventually, Virginia. In all his travels, this was the furthest west he had ever been, and he could feel his excitement building more and more. A stop at Chattanooga allowed him his first chance to walk around and have a good look. The mountains, here, were different than the ones he had seen. They were taller and with the smoke on top, they took on a blue tint that Dave had never dreamed. He had heard of the Blue Mountains to the west, but always considered it to be a metaphor. Now, he realized they were really blue and beautiful. He couldn't help but wonder how his mountains would look. Would they be blue like these? He had heard there were beautiful mountains in Maine, but he had never seen them first-hand. He still pondered these and other questions, as he took one last look, before boarding the train and settling in to continue his journey. The day was almost gone now; soon, there would be nothing to look at until morning, so settling deep in his chair, he made ready for the night.

The train bumped and ground its way on into the night and Dave managed to sleep fitfully from time to time. It made him a nervous wreck to be carrying with him the one piece of paper that carried their plans and dreams of a better life out west, but he had faith in himself and in Cabel, that they would be able to pull this off, without too much of a hitch. The weather was already starting to change, now, which meant it would soon be cold, too cold to bring in a herd this year, probably, for there would be hay to cut to feed the cattle, this winter on top of the preparations to be made just for him and Cabel to survive what was, according to August, a very cold and miserable winter. However, it would be better, if they waited, until next year to bring in a herd, anyway; they needed to learn the lay of the land around them.

Dawn was breaking now, as the train crossed out of Tennessee into the western portion of Kentucky. Shortly, they would be stopping again in Missouri. There, he would be able to find a Cabel office and check to see if there was any word from his brother.

Chapter Nine

The first streaks of the morning sun found Cabel already on the trail south out of Willow Springs. His plan was to start south and then turn east, in order to skirt around to the south of his ranch and have a look around, before continuing onto Steamboat. He had no idea what he would find, if anything, but he wanted to get an idea of the layout of the place, anyway.

"Cabel Glaize!" The voice came from someone who had just stepped out into the road and stood, now, waiting for him.

"Yeah, that's me. What do you want?" Cabel had an idea who this was that waited for him. He had stayed in Willow Springs last night, knowing his best move was to leave in the dark; however, he had nothing to hide and leaving in the middle of the night never looked good.

"My name is John Kolb and I'm the marshal here in Willow Springs. I need to talk to you, son."

He was a tall, broad shouldered man, not handsome, but stately; a man to be respected, for sure, if not feared. He wore a black boulder hat and a long black coat, one side, of which, was, now, pulled back to reveal the Colt on his right hip. He spoke with a German accent that Cabel recognized from Texas.

"I didn't shoot Slick and, to be honest, Marshal Kolb, I don't have time to argue about it."

"That's not good enough. I'll tell you what, you get on down off of that horse and let's have us a cup of coffee. But, I want to warn you now, one wrong move and it will be your last one."

Something about the way the Marshal talked, made Cabel believe this man meant what he said. Cabel had never been scared of anyone or anything, but he had never been considered a fool either.

"Alright, Marshal. Let's talk. I could use a good cup of coffee."

Cabel carefully dismounted his horse and together, the two men walked over to a spot on the side of the road and began building a fire. Once the fire was going and the makings of coffee were on, Cabel began the conversation, "Marshal, I'm not here starting trouble and I had no reason to shoot Slick Montgomery, fact is Slick just started working for me."

Marshal Kolb looked at Cabel with a puzzled look, "What do you mean, works for you?"

"We met the other night and knew each other from Missouri. He said he was ready to get shut of the Brantleys, so I offered him a job. It's that simple."

"I don't understand, son. Why would you need someone working for you? You don't even have a place to live yet, let alone a business. And it seems awful odd that the day after the shooting, you're leaving town. Why didn't you come by the saloon and talk to me last night like you had said you would do?"

"The Brantleys were in there, Tough, in particular, and I was in no mood to be railroaded into a situation I would have a hard time getting out of. Look, Marshal, I can't explain everything right now, there's too much on the line. Let's just say that the Brantleys aren't on their place legally and I know that for the truth and, soon, they are going to be very upset. Right now, I'm on my way to Steamboat to send off a message to my brother, who is on his way out here from Virginia. And if I don't get that message off, he's going to walk into one hell of a mess that he never knew existed. Now, if you want to know where I was when Slick was shot, you can go and talk to Bob Sheah. While you're at it, you can ask him about what happened to Tim Hickerson. You people seem to have put these Brantleys up on a pedestal, for some reason, but that's all about to come crashing down around you. I can't go into detail right now, for fear of endangering my brother, but in a few days, you'll see what I'm talking about. Now, as far as I know, we're not inside city limits anymore, so unless you are a federal marshal, you can't arrest me, so why don't we end this conversation and I'll go on about my business and see you in a few days?"

"You know, son, I don't care much for the Brantleys neither, but, as Marshal of this town, I have they duty to protect its citizens, all of them. So, I don't let my personal feeling get involved. However, if what you say is true, you're fixing to stir up trouble, whether you want to or not, and it's my job to shut it down, so you be careful how you go about this thing and what you do had better be legal or make no mistake, son, I'll bring you down. Now, you go on about your business, for now. I'll talk to Bob Sheah and to Slick, if he wakes up and if your stories don't match, you'd be money, ahead not to show your face around here again. And wherever you go, you had better be watching for posters. Slick was a good man and I'll get the man who shot him, whether it was you or someone else, makes no matter to me."

"Fair enough. Say, Marshal, it's none of my business, but I recognize your accent, you wouldn't have family in Texas, would you?"

"Yeah, I do and you're right. It's none of your business."

"Well, if that's all you want with me, I've got things to do. Be seeing you, Marshal," Cabel put his coffee cup down and mounting his horse, rode off. He knew that the story he had told the Marshal would hold up, once everything came out, but, right now, he could not reveal his information to any more than necessary.

He rode south for another few miles, then left the road and turned east. Within an hour or so, he should be reaching the outer edge of, what was now, the Brantley range. He would have to be careful from here on out. If he was caught out like this by the Brantleys, he would be in the same shape as Slick or worse.

Slowly, he eased his way on through the open country, staying close to the trees as much as possible, crossing each rise with care, pausing, just at the top to look over, before he crossed. He knew better than to silhouette himself against the bright blue sky and, therefore, offering himself as an easy target to anyone, who might be lying in wait for him.

Finally, he reached the foot of the mountains where the Brantley range began. Choosing his trail carefully, he rode up, toward the top in search of a place, so he could scout the country. Rounding a bend in the trail, he found a place where he could see most of the range that he was to own. The house was not visible from this spot, it was just out of sight from where he sat; however, he could see most everything surrounding it. There were several hundred head of cattle visible. What would happen to those cows, when the Brantleys left? Would they try and take the cattle with them or would they simply leave and leave them here? If they left them that would be a good start to herd he wanted; otherwise, he could still get some from someone in Steamboat.

Suddenly, movement caught his eye; nothing he could make out just yet, but enough to grab his attention. Something or someone, off to the north, was coming down into the valley; he, now, watched. As the riders came closer, he still could not make out who it was, but he could see that there were three men riding toward a draw, that was closed off from his view. The draw was not large, certainly not large enough to hold many cows. And these men were not looking for cows and they knew where they were going. If only Cabel could get around there and see what the men were riding to. He searched from his position for a way to see where the men had gone, but there was no way to get there, without being seen. Therefore, the best thing Cabel could do, for now, was to mark the place down in his mind and move on back to his horse.

Back on his horse and well on his way to Steamboat, he had time to think and try to work things out. The Brantleys controlled this range, for the time being, and with all he had been told, it wasn't really all that wonderful of a place to have. Yet, there was some reason they were so intent on holding it. Could it be that there was no special reason, just one old man wanting to settle down and figuring on doing it the easy way, with an already built house and corrals? Cabel doubted that was it, but it was a possibility. The layout on the place was good; Bob Sheah had said he would've settled there, had Williams not already been there. It was probably the best place around here, but there were much better places to settle than this. So, why? What was it about this place that Cobb Brantley wanted so badly?

As the sun was starting to set, he made his camp alongside a small creek that was flowing down from the north. He would be directly south of the main part of the ranch now. The house was located on the western most edge of the ranch land, leaving open land for several miles on the eastern side, which was where he would be right now. Of course, he had been drifting to the south at the same time, which meant he was several miles below the ranch now. But, he was trying to maintain his bearing. Tomorrow, he would reach Steamboat and get his message off to Dave and try and get some information on possibly buying some cattle in the spring. He would have to get a brand registered, also, and maybe learn something about the Brantleys, while he was there.

Dawn, again, found Cabel in the saddle. The roan gelding was in the mood to go, so Cabel let him have his head and together, they made good time. Cabel rode into Steamboat in time for lunch; his first good meal, since leaving Virginia, with the exception of the lunch he had eaten at the Sheah ranch. The waitress was a small, shapely girl with brown hair and eyes.

"I believe I'll have a steak," he stated, as the waitress walked up. "And tea, if you have it."

"If you're looking for work, you're about too late," the speaker was an older man, who had walked up to Cabel's left. He was dressed nice with a grey suit and matching hat. His boots barely showed the dust that he had picked up out on the street, "Buying and selling is about done for the year, but there might be some local work around, if you're interested."

"No, sir. Thank you, but I ain't looking for work. I'm needing information. I'm starting my own place and I'll be needing some good cattle in the spring. I was told to talk to Jack Nelson. Do you know him, by chance?"

"Yes, I know him. But, why him? Couldn't you buy cattle from anyone selling?" the man said, as he sat down.

"Coffee will be fine for me, thank you," he told the waitress, when she came over to the table.

"Yeah, I guess I could. I was just told that he was a man who I could trust. And you are?" Cabel was starting to wonder what was going on. This man had just come in, out of the blue, asking questions, talking, as if they had known each other for years. Did this man know who he was or why he was here? It was doubtful, but, at this point, Cabel was suspicious of everyone.

"Ha, ha," he laughed, "The suspicious type, I can appreciate that. You seem like the kind of man that will do well in this business or any business, for that matter. My name is Mose Dellinger and no, I don't know anything about you or your business. I'm just good at reading people. I have to be, in my business. I'm in the cattle business, myself, sort of. You see, I own, at least, a part of almost every ranch in this part of the country. Not much goes on that I don't know about, most, of which, I'm involved in. This ranch of yours, where is it? Mr...."

"Cabel Glaize and my ranch is north of here, a ways. And if you're involved in it now, don't worry yourself you won't be long. You see, I own this place fair and square, no banks involved. Now, if you'll excuse me, I would like to eat a bite and get on about my business."

"I didn't mean to insult you, Mr. Glaize. However, I should warn you, you won't have much luck with your business, without me," he explained, as he got up to leave.

Cabel watched the man, as he walked across the room and sat down at a table, near a small group of men, who, obviously, knew and recognized him. Obviously, he thought of himself as an important man and so was thought of highly by, at least, some of the inhabitants of the city. Cabel wondered, as he often did, when he met someone for the first time that who the man, really, was and what sort of business he conducted. Cabel had mentioned banking to the man, but he had not acknowledged whether or not that was his business, which led Cabel to believe he was not a banker. But if not, what then? A common thief, who had covered his tracks well over the years? There were some that had a way of doing these things and staying out of sight. Some had even reached high levels of politics and were never found out.

Cabel laid enough money on the table to pay for his meal and walked across the room to where Mose had sat down to drink his coffee and made his presence known. Leaning down to where only he and Mose would hear what was being said, he stated, frankly, "Look, Mose Dellinger or whoever you may be, I own my place fair and square, like I said. Now, I've got enough idiots telling me what I can and can't do and it's really starting to aggravate me. Now, do all involved a favor and stay out of my way and out of my business. Good day to you, now."

"From the look of your face, maybe you should listen a little better."

Cabel, who had forgotten about his fight with Lucky Parnell, suddenly remembered and the anger flushed through him, like a wave of hot water. Grabbing the man by the front of his shirt, Cabel put his face down close to Dellinger's and slowly spelled out his thoughts, "First off, the man who gave me these bruises got a couple broken ribs and a busted jaw for his trouble. Second, and make no mistake about this one, if I have to, I'll kill whoever tries to stop me from what I intend to do. I've got too much time, energy, and money involved to let some grease-ball keep me from having this. Now, the best thing you can do is get out of my way and stay out of my face."

Saying that, Cabel turned loose of Mose and walked out of the restaurant; noting, on the way out, at the faces of the men and women sitting in the room. Obviously, this man was as important, as he thought himself to be, but Cabel was in no mood to be pushed by anyone.

Outside, the afternoon had turned hot and dusty. Cabel Glaize, the one-time drifting cowhand, paused for an instant to let his eyes adjust, before moving on. The confrontation in the restaurant had angered him more than he had known, for it was true, he had worked hard to get what he had coming and there was still a lot of work left to do. He was sure that given time, he would have found out that his ranch, now in the hands of the Brantleys, was one that was under the control of this Mose Dellinger character. Well, he concluded, he was not the Brantleys and he would not be pushed around by anyone. What was his, was his and no one else's.

Cabel looked to the left and to the right. The street was busy at this time of day. Mounting his horse he rode on toward the center of town, in search of the Cabel office, which he was told was at the end of town on the left, and finding it, he walked in. The room was pleasant, as was most in town, and, again, he paused to adjust to the light, before moving on in.

"Can I help you, sir?" the speaker was a short, plump man, sitting behind the desk on Cabel's left.

"Yeah, I need to send a wire to Kansas City," Cabel answered, walking up to the desk.

"Alright, fill this out for me and I'll get it out as soon as I can. Will you be expecting an answer?" the operator asked, as he handed Cabel a paper and pen to write his message on.

"No, not really. But I'll be in town a day or two anyway, so I'll check back before I leave."

Then, he walked over to another desk and sat down to write out his message.

'TROUBLE BREWING HERE
COME QUIET AND HEELED
TRUST NO ONE
C.G.'

"Will that be all, sir?" the operator asked, as he took the paper back from Cabel.

"Yeah, that will be it. How much do I owe you?"

"Two bits'll do it. You have a nice day. If you get an answer, it'll be here when you come back."

"Alright. Thank you," and Cabel walked out of the office to conduct his other business.

Mounting his horse, he turned him back toward the way he had come and toward the Last Chance Saloon. On the street, he had a good chance to look the town over. It was truly a nice town; not as big as some, but quaint and busy. Approximately one fourth of the cattle in the country came through here, at one time or another. It was a busy time for cow towns. The railroad was making it easier for the cattlemen to ship their beef, elsewhere, in the country, which made it a more profitable business for everyone and it wasn't hard to see the profitability in this town. It was perfectly situated with Main Street, running east and west, alongside the Yampa River on the south side of the street. Tucked into the base of the mountains, it was not only a busy town, but a beautiful one as well.

At the very edge of town, Cabel found the Last Chance Saloon and after tying his horse at the hitch rail, he entered the dimly lit room. It was still early in the day for saloon business, but the place was already full. Most of the patrons were not drinking, however, but conducting business, as was the custom in the area, at the time.

After giving his eyes a few seconds to adjust, he was able to take a mental note of everyone in the room. There was no one in here that he knew, but yet he knew from experience, everyone. The years on the cow trail had taught him well, but, yet, he felt he had learned more in just the last few days than he ever had. And, now, he was learning how to use all the information he had been taught.

He had not, yet, ran into anyone he knew, but, then, it had been a couple years, since he had spent any time in this area and most of the people he knew were like him and moved around a lot. Yet, it was only a matter of time, until he ran into someone he knew and not everyone in this area was his friend. He had made a few enemies, over the years, and chances were good that some of them are still in this area.

Walking up to the bar, he ordered whiskey. Not that he cared to drink, but there was nothing else of any good to be had, at the time, and he needed to have something in front of him, while he passed the time. The bartender was the first person he recognized, but since he hadn't drank much over the last few years, he wasn't recognized in return.

After the bartender had brought his drink, Cabel got up and moved to a table back in the corner where he could watch the door. He had never met Jack Nelson, but would know from the description, given to him by Bob Sheah, when he arrived.

For what seemed like hours, Cabel sat at his table waiting, listening to the sounds of the town; the same sounds that could be heard in just about any town at that time of day and at that moment in history. The horses and buggies going up the dusty street, jingling their trace chains, as they go could be heard above all. The men and women walking up and down the boardwalk, carrying on their usual conversations could be heard, if one was paying attention. Cabel could not hear what the conversations were about, but one could guess for the conversations were all about the same. Local gossip, cattle, who is in town that everyone should know, the gold that's being found out west, and sometimes, about the fight with fists or guns that have taken place lately, were just some of the conversations that took place in towns, such as these.

Cabel sat and wondered about the Hitchens Ranch. Was he still in business? There had been some talk of the railroad coming through, when he had been here before and obviously, it had made it this far. The little town of Poole had been growing, when Cabel had left out on the stage three years ago and, now, with the railroad coming through, it must've really grown. It had started much like any other town at that time; someone had come through and stopped, due to the hole of water that was there; thus, the name 'Poole'. Then, slowly, over time, more had stopped and built houses and ranches, until a town started to develop. Eventually, they built schools and a post office. This one in particular had also been a favorite stop for the stage partly, due to the cooking of Mrs. Hitchens and some of the other ladies that inhabited the town. Cabel would have to go see Hitchens, before he made a deal with anyone else. Hitchens had always liked Cabel, for he was a hardworking young man and had performed well, when employed, at the ranch. He may be able to make a better deal for a herd, there, than he could with anyone else. It was worth a try, anyway.

The last couple of days and the ride to Steamboat were starting to take its toll on Cabel. He was getting tired and sleepy and that meant careless. He had been waiting for almost two hours and had seen no one he knew or matching the description of Jack Nelson. He was about to get up to leave, when he though he heard a familiar voice, out on the walk.

"Yeah, we'll go to the land office tomorrow. But, right now, I want a drink," the first voice said.

"Me, too. Man I feel rough," came an answer. Both voices were plain now and easily recognizable to Cabel.

"You should feel bad, Lucky, you got your ass whipped," Tough laughed, as they walked through the front door of the Last Chance Saloon.

"Oh yeah, keep up that mouth, Tough, and you'll get a chance to see how I feel first-hand," Lucky wasn't amused by Tough's humor in the least.

"Awe, I'm just teasin' you, Lucky. Get over it. His time's coming. He'll get what we should've given to Slick. I still can't believe he got away from us, like he did."

The shadows had started to fall now and the bar was not yet lit inside, therefore, Cabel was hidden well in the shadows, when the two entered the saloon. So, they had yet to notice him sitting there, as they walked through the doors and up to the bar and Cabel was just about to rise and have a talk with them, when the doors swung open and in walked a man matching the description of Jack Nelson.

Although Cabel wanted to have a talk with Tough Brantley and Lucky Parnell, it would have to wait until another time. But, now, how would he get Jack's attention, without also gaining the unwanted attention of the two Brantley men? Cabel decided he would just have to wait and hope that the two troublemakers would leave or if not, he would just have to risk it.

Jack Nelson fit the description to a tee that Cabel had been given; yet, there was something more; something that could not be described. There was an air about the man that seemed to tell everyone around him who he was and how important he was and, also, how dangerous he would be, if crossed. *"This would be a good man to have on your side, if things got rough,"* Cabel decided as he watched the man cross the room and sit down at a table in the far-right corner, from where Cabel, now, sat.

Jack was not a big man, as far as weight. He was tall; probably, all of six feet and six inches, but probably no more than two hundred pounds. His broad shoulders were starting to show the years of life the man had lived and Cabel could only imagine the type of life the man had led. Jack wore his gun tied low on his right hip, ready for action, even though the two men that moved along with him looked able enough to handle any problem that might arise. However, it was obvious that Jack Nelson was used to trouble and, also, able to handle it.

The saloon was starting to fill up now and with the patrons filling the room, it was getting loud. Cabel decided if he was going to conduct any business, it would have to happen soon and there was no better way to handle it than just walking over and introducing himself.

The two Brantley men were still at the bar, with their backs turned to Cabel, when he got up from his table and starting making his way across the room where Jack Nelson sat drinking with his two companions keeping a steady watch over the room.

One, two, three steps across the room, expecting at any time for the Brantleys to turn and recognize him, before he could reach his destination. The confrontation was going to happen, eventually; right now, however, was not the time, in which, he wanted it. He had business here to take care of, then he needed to return to Willow Springs, and get started taking back what was rightfully his.

"Almost there," Cabel thought to himself, almost at the same time he heard Lucky Parnell's voice ring out, "Hey, Tough! Lookie here, I think we've found us a rat."

Cabel stopped in his tracks and turned to face the two men, who were now turned and staring in his direction.

"I ain't got time for it, boys. I've got business to tend to. I'll deal with you two, when we get home," he said slowly and calmly, wanting to go ahead and take care of it right now, if for no other reason than to get it out of the way. But this really wasn't a good time.

"No, Cabel Glaize. I think we'll deal with this right here, right now," Tough said, as he moved away from the bar and was fading over toward Cabel's left. Lucky was also moving, but he was going to Cabel's right. It was plain what was about to happen. They were about to box him in.

"Cabel Glaize?" the voice came from behind him. It was Jack Nelson, who spoke now, "I hear you're looking to talk to me."

Cabel, not wanting to take his eyes off the pair in front of him, returned the conversation, "Yes, sir. I wanted to talk to you about the possibility of buying a herd to take to Willow Springs, but, right now, I've got a couple of horse flies buzzing around that I need to slap."

"Well, turn around here and have a seat. I don't think those boys will bother you. Will you, boys?"

He was talking to the Brantleys, but it was his own two guards that moved to step between Cabel and his adversaries.

"No, sir. They ain't gonna bother nobody," the one on the right said. Just for a second, one could see the want in Tough's eyes, but, eventually, his judgment took over and he turned and walked back to the bar; mumbling something about another day and Cabel knew it was going to be a long ride back to Willow Springs.

Chapter Ten

"Look, lady, as much as I would love to lay here and look at your beautiful face, I've got work to do. If what you say is true, then I need to go talk to some people and let them know what is going on," Slick Montgomery was serious about staying there looking at the young Miss Williams, but was, also, serious about what else he had to do. He had been shot on his way from the Brantley Ranch and someone had been going around telling everyone that Cabel had committed the shooting. Slick had no idea whether or not what he said would do any good, for he had only been in this country for a short period of time and had not spent much time at all in town, therefore, no one really knew much about him, other than he worked, or did work, for Brantley.

"Mr. Montgomery…" Kimberly was blushing, even though she didn't want to, over the comment Slick had made, "You're not well enough, yet, to be up and around. Your wounds haven't healed and if you get them to bleeding again, you could very well bleed to death, if you're not close enough to town to get there."

She knew she was telling him the truth, but she really shouldn't care, should she? Well, yes, she should. She did work for the doctor and for that reason alone, she should care what happened to her patients. But was that the only reason? She felt as though it wasn't, but told herself that was the only reason, for even though she didn't know this man, she did know of him and didn't like what she had heard.

"Miss Williams, I appreciate your concern and I promise I'll stay close and out of trouble. I'll go and talk to the Marshal and I'll come straight back and we'll have lunch. How does that sound?" Slick had seen the look of real concern in the girl's eyes and was playing all the cards at his disposal.

"Mr. Montgomery, I didn't... I mean I... Oh, just go, if that's what you want. I never said I wanted to have lunch with you. I was just concerned for your health, that was all," she explained, trying to act, as though, she was offended by the frankness of his statement. Then, as an added punctuation to her act, she turned and walked out of the room.

Slick got up and dressed with a smile on his face, knowing he had made an impression and he vowed he would be back in time to, at least, invite her out to lunch, whether she went or not. But, for right now, there was work that had to be done. The Marshal and no doubt, half the town, now, thought that Cabel had shot him. He had to tell what he knew. He knew that they would probably not believe him, for they thought highly of the Brantleys. But, some way, he must, at least, make them understand that Cabel was not guilty.

These things were on his mind, as he reached for the front door and caused him to remember what had happened and that if word got out of who had actually done the shooting, then the Brantleys would have a lot to lose. He would have to be careful who he talked to and every step from this point on would go with danger. He knew the Brantleys well enough to know that if there was anything they could do, he would not live long enough to tell the story.

Pausing now, at the front door, Slick decided it would be better to use the back, that way he would be able to slip, along the alley ways to the Marshal's office. The way would be good, until he had to cross the street. Would the Brantleys try for him in broad daylight? Slick wondered, as he opened the back door to peer out at the valley that surrounded Willow Springs.

The sun was bright in his eyes after the last few days of being inside, so he let his eyes adjust, before moving out of the door and into the open. So far, no one knew he was up and around, except for Kimberly and she had not left the house, so they would not be expecting him around town. He had to get to the Marshal's office and let him know what the Brantleys were doing and that Cabel Glaize was the true owner of the ranch. That would help explain why Cabel was here and take, at least, some of the heat off of him, as he went about his business.

Slick crept along the back street, going from house to house, ducking under the windows as best as he could with his leg. Although he could walk, every step caused him pain and he could feel his wounds trying to pull open with every step. Just one more house, then he would turn left into the alley that would come out on the street, just across from the Marshal. As he reached the alley, all looked clear, so he turned and eased his way through the various barrels and boxes that were stacked in his way to the street. There, he peered out from around the corner, back toward the heart of town. The office was located on the north end of town; therefore, from where he, now, stood, he could see all the way down Main Street.

The building he was beside, was Farley's General Store. Next to that was the Dipsy Doodle, then the various other buildings that are commonly found in western towns. As he looked, he noticed the two Brantley horses tied at the hitching rail in front of the Doodle. So, they were in town then. Were they here waiting for him to wake up? Or were they just in town for a drink? At this time of day, they should have something to do, other than this, for he knew that Cobb, if nothing else, believed in keeping his employees busy. If they were here, it was for a reason and that reason was probably to keep Slick from talking. As he thought, two men walked out of the saloon and stood on the walk. From where, Slick was now standing, he could not see who it was, but, from the look, it was the two Brantleys. They stood together, talking quietly, as they looked off in the direction of the doctor's office.

So, they were here waiting for him then. How could he cross the street, without being seen? Even if he were not injured, he would never be able to make it, but, now, he could barely walk and to make matters worse, he could feel his leg starting to swell. He needed to be back at the doctor's office in bed, but to turn back, now, would be a wasted trip, aside from the fact that Cabel was innocent and only he knew it. He glanced at his watch, ten-thirty. What he needed was a diversion of some sort. Something to draw their attention elsewhere, long enough for him to get across the street and into the Marshal's office.

Suddenly, the noise of a buckboard, coming down the dusty street, caught his attention. As he turned, he recognized the occupants at once. It was the Sheahs. What a stroke of luck. He had found his diversion and some friends, at the same time. Of course, the Sheahs had no idea, as of yet that they were friends, but that would soon be remedied. The Brantley men had noticed the Sheahs as well and all their attention was, now, centered in that direction. In just a few more minutes, the Sheahs would stop, probably at Farley's, and that's when he would move. Even as the thought was coming to him, the wagon was slowing to stop, and the Brantley men were watching closely to see what Bob Sheah would do.

Bob had seen the Brantley crew in front of the saloon, as soon as he rounded the corner into town. He had, also, noticed Slick Montgomery in the alley next to Farley's. He had not heard of the shooting yet, but he remembered what Cabel had said about Slick quitting the Brantleys and wondered then, if it was true. Why else would Slick be hiding from them? Or was he? Could he be hiding in the alley waiting on the Sheahs to come into town? Why would he be? No one outside his bunch knew they were coming today and after the shooting, no one was expecting them. So, maybe it was true then. Slick Montgomery had left the Brantleys and was, now, once again, on the good side of the law.

"Keep your eyes open, boys. There's trouble brewing here," Bob told Will and Sandy, as he got down from the rig with his rifle in hand. Will and Sandy had, yet, to forget about their friend, Tim, still lying in his bed, fighting for his life. The doctor had been brought out to check on him, but the bullet had passed through, so there was nothing he could do that Mrs. Sheah hadn't already done. So, he left them to hope and pray and they had been doing plenty of that. But Tim was slowly improving, so it was looking good.

"Bob, I believe we can take them right now. How about a little payback?" Will said, as he stared toward the two Brantley men walking toward them.

"Yeah, Will, we probably could, but everything up to this point is hearsay. You start shooting now and all anyone will see is that you started it. Let's just wait. Out turn will come," Bob had noticed the two men walking in their direction and wanted no trouble now, but he would, if, at all possible, distract them long enough to let Slick go ahead with whatever business he was trying to conduct.

"You two need to just go on about your business and leave us alone. We didn't come here for a fight, but we'll damn sure give you one, if that's what you want."

"Awe, now, come on, old man. We was just wanting to talk. You know, just visit. Get all neighborly like," Frank Lawton said, as he eased closer to the buckboard. This wasn't the reason they had been sent into town, but the boss would sure be happy, if they were able to run Bob Sheah out of business and, besides, Slick was still laid up in the doctor's office.

Frank and his younger brother, Tommy, were noted for staying in trouble. They had ridden with several gangs and generally stayed in some sort of mischief, since leaving home, at the ages of sixteen and fourteen. However, in ten years of traveling, neither had ever received the reputation they had wanted for being bad men. They had though, earned reputations as trouble. No one was scared of them, but everyone knew that where the Lawtons went, trouble wasn't far behind.

"We ain't in no mood to talk right now, boys. We've got work to do. Ever hear that word, work? You know, earning your way, instead of letting someone else do the work and then you moving your sorry ass in and chasing them off at gun point."

"I tell you what, Will Kollet, you get down off of that wagon and talk to me like that and I'll show you what work is, you loudmouth son-of-a-bitch!" Tommy was getting angry now. After all the years of running with Frank, he had nothing to show for his troubles, but, maybe, a wanted poster or two. Frank had promised him riches everywhere they went, but none had proved true and, now, he had nothing. Also, he knew that most of what Will had said was true and he resented the fact that people thought that way about him. He had always been considered a hardworking kid, before he had left home with Frank. But, over the years, that had changed and now, he was starting to realize what his life had amounted to and Tommy was not happy with what he saw, when he looked in the mirror.

"Will! You stay put. We don't have time for this foolishness. We need to get our supplies and get on back."

Bob knew that Will was anxious to fight either man, but, now, was truly not the time. Bob was not only worried about his boys getting into trouble but was also worried about leaving his wife and daughter at home, alone. With the Brantleys around, anything could happen.

"Frank Lawton!" The booming voice from across the street was easily heard and easily recognized.

"I know you boys ain't stirring up trouble here in Willow Springs. I would sure hate to have to arrest y'all right here in broad daylight."

"Why no, Marshal Kolb. We was just having a friendly conversation with ol' Bob and his boys here."

Frank knew it was not a good idea to lock horns with John Kolb. John had a reputation of being one of the best men in this part of the country, but also one of the meanest, when crossed and he had proven several times in the past.

"Well, then, why don't you boys go and have you a conversation somewhere else. It looks to me like these boys have work to do," the Marshal said, as he walked up to the wagon.

"Yes sir, Marshal. We was all just getting mighty thirsty anyway. Come on, Tommy; let's go get us a drink. We'll catch up to these boys another time," Frank was talking to Tommy, but looking at Will and each man, within earshot, knew what it was Frank had meant by the comment.

"Yeah, we'll talk another time, Frank. Maybe, have us a private conversation, just you and me. What do you think?" Will said with a grin, wishing that he were away from here, so he and Frank could settle this feud between them once and for all.

Neither Frank nor Tommy commented, they just smiled, as they turned and walked toward the door of the Dipsy Doodle.

"Thanks, John. I didn't know how much longer I was going to be able to keep Will off of them boys. There's big trouble coming and you know how Will is. He's not one to wait around for someone else to drop the hat. If you know what I mean," Bob said, as the two men shook hands.

"Yeah, I've heard. Had a little talk with Cabel Glaize yesterday, you know him?"

"Met him. Can't say I know him. We had a run in with Tough and his boys, although we can't prove it was them. Next day, Cabel comes in and helps gather our stock and get us back to the ranch. You know though, Sandy Pearson says he knows him; has for several years. Says they rode together for a while back in Texas. Sandy says he'll stand for him and if Sandy says, it I'll believe him."

"I'll stand for him myself."

No one had noticed Slick, as he slowly made his way out of the alley and onto the walkway.

"I'll also stand for what Bob says about the fight they had with the Brantleys. I wasn't there, but I met up with them right afterwards; heard them bragging about it. Fact is that's why I quit. I didn't sign on for that kind of action. I'm wanting to clear my name, not ruin it."

"Yeah, I heard you quit. So, I guess you're here to tell me it wasn't Cabel Glaize, who put those leaks in you then," Marshal Kolb was starting to get a mental picture of what was going on in his quiet little town and liked none of it.

"No sir, it wasn't. It was Tough Brantley and his boys. Didn't see 'em, but I did hear and recognize their voices."

Then, after a moment of thought, "Cabel Glaize is a good man, Marshal. Fact is I've thrown in with him and his brother, when he gets here. They've got a legal claim to that place. The Brantleys ain't gonna like it none, but that's the way it is, when you want to take advantage of someone else's hard work."

"Alright, Slick. You've said your piece. I'll need to think on this for a while. Meanwhile, you had better get back to the doc's. You don't look like you got any business out here, right now. I'll be by to talk to you some more later."

With that, Slick turned and was going back down the alley, the way he had come, headed back toward the doctor's office to rest and finish healing, as much as he would be able, before the real trouble started; leaving the Marshal and Bob Sheah, alone, to finish the conversation.

"I don't like the feel of it, Bob. I know that if Cabel does have legal title to the Williams place, then the law says it's his, but this gonna get ugly."

"Yeah, I know what you mean, John. That's why I'm here today. 'Cause, when Cabel gets back from Steamboat it ain't gonna be safe to travel around here, till this is settled."

Bob Sheah started to walk off toward the store to help the others gather and load the goods they would need in the weeks to come but an afterthought came to him and he turned back to the Marshal, who was still standing there, apparently deep in his own thoughts.

"One thing bothers me, though. Kimberly is old man Williams' niece. Why didn't she speak up, when the Brantleys were trying to find him? Seems to me she would know where to find him."

With that, Bob continued on with his business, eager to get back to his ranch, in case of trouble. Marshal Kolb, even more alone now than ever before, made his way across the street and back to his office.

Since taking this job, it had been quiet, easy even. With only the occasional drunk to contend with or the usual trouble that could be found in town, all across the west. This was shaping up, however, to be quite a bit more than he was used to. More than he could handle? Maybe, maybe not; but one thing for sure, if he couldn't handle it, he knew people who could. The town's people would be of no great use, for most of them liked the Brantleys and the others were scared of them. Also, Cabel was a stranger and like them or not, everyone knew the Brantleys. There were men, he could contact, that would come and help, but that, too, was a last resort. He knew that, in the west, men were expected to fight their own battles and especially, once you put that star on your chest. He was not in this yet, but he knew it was only a matter of time, now, before all hell broke loose in his quiet little town.

Back in his office, he sat down and considered what he knew. Cobb Brantley had made a legitimate attempt to get the proper paperwork on the Williams property, when he moved in or so it had seemed. Surely, he would have talked to Kimberly, the former owner's niece. And if he had, why would she not have told him where her uncle could be found?

Another thing that kept entering his mind is why would the Brantleys attack Bob Sheah? They had never had any trouble that he was aware of, but yet, Bob and Slick, both, agreed that the attack had come from the

Brantleys. Also, Bob was not involved in this deal with Cabel Glaize, even if he were, the attack happened before Cabel arrived, didn't it?

Things just weren't adding up. Some of the pieces were coming together, *yes*, but in a way that just made it all more confusing. Also, it was making Cobb Brantley look more like a two-bit outlaw than the cattleman that he claimed. He would need to have a talk with Cobb, to see, if there was something he was missing about when he took over the Williams ranch.

However, Cabel Glaize had produced no papers or proof of any kind that he was telling the truth; with the exception of knowing the man's name, who had previously owned that place. But that would be easy enough to find out or would it? Cobb Brantley found out, but only after he had gotten to town. Actually, after he had moved in, but could never locate the owner. Even still, what if it was Cabel, who had everyone fooled around here? What if his story about the papers was all a lie, in an attempt to move in on the Brantleys? Did he, as Marshall, have the right to go asking questions of a man whom he knew, when he had no idea, if what Cabel was claiming was even true? No, not right now. That may make things even worse than they already were. As it stands, Cobb knows nothing about Cabel having legal ownership and the longer it stayed that way, the better off everyone would be. Cabel will have to produce those papers, when he makes his claim and that will have to wait, until the arrival of his brother from Virginia. How long would that take, he wondered; a few days or maybe weeks? A lot can happen in that amount of time, a whole lot. He would have to wait and take his chances, but one thing is for sure; he would keep a close eye on all those involved.

Chapter Eleven

"Yeah, sure, three hundred head of mixed stuff, I can do that. It will take me a sometime though and this being toward the end of the season, it might not be the best of the lot. You want to pay now or pay later?" Jack Nelson asked. The young man, he saw before him, was impressive, to say the least. Not just in his size, but in his manner. The way he carried himself; straight and with a purpose. This would be a man to contend with, if push came to shove. A good man to have on your side, when trouble came. But they were also talking about nine hundred dollars' worth of cattle and Jack Nelson was not a man to play around with, when it came to money. There was a reason he always had his guards with him.

"I'll pay, when I see the cattle, if that's okay with you. No disrespect, sir, but we are talking about a considerable amount of money."

"Yes, we are, son. So, where will I find you, when I've got the cattle together?"

"I'll be around. I've got to go visit an old friend, while I'm this close, but I will be back in a day or two. I'll look you up."

Cabel had made his deal and a fair one, at least. He would soon be the proud owner of three hundred head of cattle with nowhere to put them. At least, not for now. Cabel drew a silent deep breath, as he stood to shake hands, thinking to himself that after this, there was no backing out. It was all or nothing. When the going got tough, as he knew it would, there would be no thought of quitting or getting away. This was it, then, and with that thought in his mind, he shook hands with Jack Nelson and sealed his fate, whatever that fate may turn out to be.

Now, his mind was back on the task at hand. He had a good-sized herd to get back into the Wyoming territory and no one to help him. But that was one of the reasons he was going to see Mr. Hitchens. He would still have on some extra help that would be ready to start looking for other things to do and other places to winter, with a little luck, he would be able to hire some help, for he, not only had to get them back, but there was plenty of work to do, once they arrived.

"As soon as you get the herd together, I'll get you a bank draft, but, for right now, I've got work to do."

"I'll say you do, don't forget, you've got two jobs, right behind you that have been patiently waiting for you to finish your business," Jack said with a sinister grin. He figured to find out, right now, if he was going to have to gather those three hundred head of cattle or not. That short one there, ain't that Tough Brantley, Cobb Brantley's boy? Watch him close, son, he's huntin' him a reputation, although I don't think he's man enough to earn it. I've known his father for several years, used to be a good man, but something happened to him, I don't know what. Now, he ain't of much use to anyone, other than himself or those wanting to take the easy way. Now that he's taken sick, I guess, Tough is running the show or wanting to."

"Sick, what do you mean?" Cabel had his interest up now; he knew of no reason why, but something inside was telling him this could be the break he was needing.

"I don't rightly know, son, and hate to try to say for fear of being made a liar, but from what I hear, it ain't none too good for the old man. By the way, son, if you don't mind my asking, where are you taking all these cattle? A man has to have a pretty healthy spread to accommodate three hundred head."

"Well, sir, no disrespect but, at this point, I do mind. At this point, I have a bunch of trouble ahead of me and don't really care to make it any worse…yet."

Jack Nelson let out a wide knowing grin and motioned to his men that the business between himself and Cabel Glaize was, now, concluded. Then after a hearty handshake, the guards turned to allow Cabel room to leave the table. However, as Cabel moved to push his chair back under the table, he suddenly pulled it out and as he turned, flung it toward the two men at the bar, who had been waiting for him to conclude his business. The chair was true to its mark, Lucky, who was not paying attention, was struck with a loud crack on the back of the knee and was immediately down and out of the equation. In an instant, the way between Cabel and Tough was cleared and all noise and conversation had ceased. Everyone had seen and felt the tension between these two men and had heard the crack of breaking bones, when the chair had struck his mark. There was no doubt, as to what was about to take place now. There would be a gun battle, for that was the normal course of action, for this period of time. And with all the talk that the smaller man had been talking, it would be a sure and quick thing.

"All right, you little turd, you have been stirring up trouble for me, ever since I rode into this part of the country. Now, is your chance to back it up," Cabel stated, as he stood and glared at Tough, feet shoulder width apart and hands at the ready. Cabel had never considered himself to be a fast draw, although he knew he was probably as fast as any. He just never wanted the reputation. For along with the reputation, came the reputation hunters. And the better your reputation was, the more you had to prove you deserved it, which meant it was kill or be killed. But, right now, he had been pushed to his limits and although no one knew how fast he was, he was just in the mood to show it.

The onlookers in the room had not moved nor had a word been spoken. This short, young man had braced his adversary, then backed down for Jack Nelsons men, but had continued to talk; to tell everyone what he would do to the man he hated. But, now, facing the man, he had changed. His attitude had changed; even the once proud look in his eyes was no longer there. There was still hatred, but also something else, fear. After all the talk about beating his adversary, he was suddenly quiet. His friend was now out of commission and no longer of any help, but, surely, after all the talk, he would make his move, isn't this the chance he was looking for? This was Cobb Brantley's son, Tough, wasn't it? Nearly everyone knew him and those that knew him, thought of him as a bad man. Surely everyone wasn't wrong. Now was his chance to prove that he was what he had claimed to be. But why was he just standing there? Who was this stranger, anyway? He had come in from off of the street to meet with Jack Nelson, obviously for the first time, to buy some cattle. Now, here, he was facing down Tough Brantley, in front of everyone.

If it had not been for the ticking of the clock in the corner, Cabel would have bet that time had stopped. How long had he stood there? Surely, only a few seconds, but it felt like an eternity.

"Aw to hell with this," Cabel stated, as he took the few steps across the room to come face to face with Tough Brantley.

Tough tried to take a step backward, but was stopped by the bar against his back.

"Next time you decide to brace me, you little bastard, you had better be ready to back it up or I might just shoot you for being a coward. Now is your chance, make your move or get the hell out of my way. I have business to tend to," Cabel said, when he was so close their noses almost touched.

"Your day is coming, Cabel Glaize, I'll kill you before all of this is over," Tough got the words out but with a struggle, for by this time more than just fear was choking him, it was also the shame of being man handled, in front of all these people, after he had talked so much. After all, he was somebody. He was Tough Brantley, everyone knew that and everyone knew not to buck what he said, except for this stranger. Who was he, anyway, where did he come from? Tough knew he had never been afraid of anyone, yet there was something about this man that sent a warning deep into his soul. Just, now, he had felt that feeling in the pit of his stomach; the one that you get, when falling or when you walk up on a snake in the grass. He was scared of this man. Though he had no reason, he was scared. Tough knew then and there that no matter, what, or how, he would have to get rid of Cabel Glaize.

"Look, Tough, I ain't hardly slept in a week. I'm tired and ornery and too busy to stand here and exchange pleasantries with you, so either make your move or get the hell out of my way."

Everything Cabel had said was the truth. He was in no mood to stand and argue or play around with Tough Brantley or any of his gang, for that matter. All he wanted, now, was to get on with his business and get out of town with his cattle and up into the hanging valley, before the snow got too deep. Dave should be rolling in any day now and Cabel wanted to, at least, have made somewhat of a showing by that time.

Tough Brantley made no move to attack or even speak, the confidence this man held was enough to raise caution and everyone in the place could see it. Everyone knew that one false move, at this time, would be the last move made by Tough Brantley.

The moments passed like hours, with a fear and resentment hanging over the whole room like a rain cloud.

"Just what I thought, Tough, you got no heart. Get the hell out of my way. I've got work to do," then, without turning to look, "Mr. Nelson, I will see you in a few days."

And Cabel Glaize walked out of the Last Chance Saloon, mounted his horse, and headed west, out of town, to continue with the rest of the business at hand.

Cabel was a little upset with himself, at this point, he had let his feelings get involved in the conversation with Tough. He had said too much and knew it and, now, if Tough is smart enough to put two and two together, everyone will know why he is here. And that will, for sure, complicate things even more.

"Oh well, to hell with them. They're going to find out soon enough as it is. Might as well get it over with," he said aloud to himself, as he rode into the now setting sun to see his old friend and former boss, Albert Hitchens. He didn't notice Mose Dellinger sitting at a table in the corner of the room, as he walked out, and he certainly didn't notice that after he left, Mose got up and went to sit at the bar, next to Tough Brantley. And no one but the two of them knew what their conversation was about.

The hour and a half or so ride allowed Cabel some time to think about his plan and how he should execute it. He had bought some cows and had a place, at least temporary, to put them up for the winter, but there was hay that needed to be cut and, of course, there was also shelter that would be needed for himself and Dave. Dave should be showing up any day now. Cabel wondered had he received the message that was sent about the trouble that was sure to get stirred up. Everything had sounded so easy, when they purchased the land from Mr. Williams, back east. But, of course, things are never as easy as they seem and Cabel had actually warned Dave that there could very easily be problems, once they entered the area. Dave, while he was street-wise, had not traveled out west as Cabel had. He knew, for sure, how underhanded men could be, but it was different out here. Things were handled in a different manner. Where there was no law, men out here tended to take matters into their own hands. Sometimes, this was a good thing and, sometimes, it was not. It just depended on who it was. A good man would handle things one way, usually the way it should be. But, then, there were the others. The men like Brantley, that knew there was no one to stop them, so they took that to mean there were no boundaries. That is, until they ran across someone who could stop them.

The hanging valley he intended on keeping the cattle in would work, but only for the time being. The grass had been growing there for several years, without being disturbed by more than the deer and elk. So, it had grown tall and thick. However, it would not sustain the cattle through next spring and summer, which meant that all of this mess would have to be settled by spring. That could be accomplished, that is, if he could accomplish it all. Everything considered, it meant, it would go one way or the other by spring. He and his brother would either be living on the land they had bought and paid for, working their cattle getting ready to sell calves or they would be dead. That realization put things into a new perspective. He would have to be more careful. Up to this point, he had just went in head first, like he always had, but thinking about it this way made him understand that his actions and reactions were going to have to be carefully thought out from this point forward.

Chapter Twelve

Tim Hickerson's eyes opened with a start. The last he remembered he was in a fight, out on the trail. He tried to sit up, before he realized he was back at the house. They must have found a way to get him back. As he remembered, both of the horses had been killed at the start of the fight, if you could call it that. It was more of an ambush. It had to be the Brantleys. Looking around the room, he saw Mrs. Sheah, asleep in the chair across the room. He was terribly thirsty, but he didn't want to wake her. Looking out the window, told him it was still dark outside and the quietness in the house let him know everyone was still asleep. The pain in his side was almost unbearable, but he was alive, that was what mattered now. Easing himself to a sitting position on the side of the bed, he was able to get both feet on the floor. He had never been shot before. And, at this point, didn't care to have it happen again. He missed his printing press about right now. *"Writing news articles is a lot easier on the body,"* he thought, as the pain stabbed his side, as he started to stand up.

"What are you doing? You get yourself back in that bed, Tim Hickerson. I just got the bleeding stopped and you're gonna get it going again. What do you need? Some water?"

"Yes, ma'am, that would be great. I apologize for waking you. I surely didn't mean to."

"You don't worry about that; it's about time for me to get up, anyway. I'll be right back with some water."

After she left the room, he was thinking, once again, about his printing press. He must get that going again. He had to get the story out about the things that were going on out here. There were constantly cattle being rustled, there had been several mysterious deaths, including the one he had written about, that caused him to have to leave town to begin with. And all had happened, since the Brantley bunch came to the valley. Maybe, if he could, at least, get some of it reported in a newspaper, it would gather enough attention to get some more law out here. The town sheriff was a good man, but he would hardly venture out on the prairie. He had enough to keep him busy in town.

"Here you go, son," Mrs. Sheah said, as she entered the room, "You drink this. I am going to go and start breakfast. I will bring you a plate, when it is done."

The water was cool, crisp, and relaxing. It didn't take long before Tim's eyes were trying to close again, as he listened to the sounds of dishes rattling in the kitchen, as breakfast was being prepared for the people he had come to think of as family. He was alive, he was home, and all was good with the world. It was, with this thought in his head that he drifted back off to sleep.

It wasn't often that Sarah Sheah showed emotion, but this was one of those times. In the kitchen, all alone with her thoughts, she quietly thanked the Lord that Tim had finally awakened. For two days and nights, she had sat with him, praying that he would survive, and her prayers had worked. These boys that worked for them had become part of an extended family to her and Bob. They thought of each and every one of them as their own children. She felt the same pain when one of them was hurt, as she did, when Amanda was hurt. The thought of losing one of them was unbearable to her and the thought of losing one to the Brantleys made matters even worse. These were cold, ruthless, heartless people. Each and every one of them would be hanged by now, had they been back east. But the reality was, they were not back east, so they would either have to endure the pain or figure out a way to stop it. And, at this point, she knew Bob had endured about all he was going to. That was the thing that scared her most, for she knew Bob very well, and knew that once he started, he wouldn't stop, until the job was finished or until he was dead.

"Any word on Tim?" Bob's voice behind her, although familiar, startled her, as she was deep in thought.

"Yes, actually, he woke up early this morning," she replied, as her husband came into the kitchen for his morning coffee and breakfast.

"Well, good, I was starting to seriously worry about that young man," he said, as he poured his coffee.

'Bob, what is your take on the gentleman that helped ya'll get home after the attack? You think he's honest? He said he knew Sandy Pearson, but I haven't talked to Sandy about him."

"He seems honest enough to me. I would think he was a young man that was willing and able to handle whatever came his way. Although, I think he may have bit off a little more than he can chew."

"Yea, I told him that very thing, but he seems like he is more than willing to do what needs to be done, when the time comes. He does seem like a good, young man, though. I hope he gets through this."

"Well, Sarah, I guess we'll just have to wait and see what happens. I will help the boy any way I can, as long as he continues to show that he's honest and straight forward. But what has you thinking about him, anyway?"

"Oh, I don't know, Bob. I guess just because he seems like such a nice man, but with such a hard task ahead of him. If he makes it through, he would make a good addition this area. You know the Brantleys have kept this country beat down for so long. It would be nice to see it start to recover, you know, build itself back up."

"Who are ya'll talking about? Sounds like someone I need to meet," Sandy Pearson had entered the room during the conversation, without anyone hearing.

"Oh, good morning, Sandy," Sarah said, upon hearing his voice, "Actually, he says he already knows you. Something about punching cows together in Arkansas. Do you know a Cabel Glaize?"

"Cabel Glaize, here? Well, shoot, yea, I know him. What the world is he doing around here? Last I heard he was headed back east," he was completely surprised to hear the name, but it was obvious from the first that he was excited as well. He and Cabel had spent many hours eating trail dust, as they moved cows from pasture to pasture or lot to lot. Many nights out on the trail, cooking on an open fire and just talking, with nothing else to do, they would just talk. About horses, cows, land, and sometimes, about girls, as most young men did. But mostly about the other things, for they both figured the girls would come along eventually, but neither was ready, at the time, to settle down, so there wasn't much need in contemplating on it. They had become good friends in the time they worked together. Cabel was one of the only people Sandy knew he could trust completely. He was a hard worker and trustworthy. He did have a way, from time to time, of rubbing people wrong by his gruff way of talking. But, one thing was for sure, he told you the truth. It might not be what you wanted to hear, but it was always the truth.

This and more he explained to Bob and Sarah, as he ate his breakfast. It would be good to see Cabel again.

"I need you to do me a favor, Sandy," Bob said, once he had heard what Sandy had to say about his old friend, "I need you to make a trip up to the hanging valley and start getting it ready to hold a few hundred cows over the winter. Cabel has gone to Steamboat to get the makings of a herd and will need somewhere to store them, while he works out some problems. Would you mind doing that for me?"

"No, sir, anything you need. How far you want me to go to getting it ready? You want the hay cut or just leave it up? It probably should be cut and stacked. And some sort of shelter built, at least one to last the winter. Once the snow hits, there won't be any getting out till spring."

"Do whatever you think needs to be done. He should be rolling in here in a week or two, depending on if he runs into trouble."

With that, Bob pushed away his plate, got up from the table and walked toward the door, pausing there for a second, "You may better take some help with you, in case there's trouble."

With the last word being said, Bob walked out the front door and headed to the stable for his horse.

"So, Mrs. Sheah, what is going on? Is Cabel planning on settling in the hanging valley? I sort of had plans or that place myself. But I guess if Mr. Sheah has sold it, I guess I need to start looking for something else."

"No, son, it is still yours, if you want it, but Cabel needs somewhere to hold cattle for the winter. If things work out, he will have somewhere to put them in the spring. But that is a conversation I will let you have with Cabel, when he gets back."

"Ok, works for me, I guess. I'll get the place ready for him and talk to him, when he arrives then. Right now, I guess I better get started, there is a lot of work to get that valley ready."

With that, Sarah was once again left to herself in the kitchen.

Within the hour, Sandy Pearson was on his way to the hanging valley. His choice of help was Will Kollett, whose parents had come over from Germany, while his mother was still pregnant with him, but by the time he was five, he had been orphaned. His mother had become pregnant very late in life and that, in itself, took a huge toll on her health. The trip over had all but sealed the deal for her and unfortunately, she had died giving birth to him. His father, although, originally a good man, had taken the death of his wife very hard and, in turn, started drinking heavily.

Shortly after Wills fifth birthday, he had disappeared, and even, as of now, at nineteen, Will had never found out what had happened. He had been found by young couple, while wandering the streets and after spending a considerable amount of time working with the authorities to find out who he belonged to, to no avail, they had adopted him. Raising him as their own, they taught him all the things a young gentleman should learn. He had manners and respect, he could easily fit in in the fancy restaurants around New Orleans, but with his work ethic, he fit in just as well in the cow towns and out on the trail. He preferred this to the restaurants and high-class gathering places, anyway. Out here, in the open, he could relax. With no pressure on what clothes he wore or how he presented himself or even, talked. He would be forever grateful to his adopted parents for all they had done for him, however, at the age of fifteen, he had left in the night. Leaving only a note thanking them for all their help and support and explaining that, like his father, he had to make his own way in the world. He drifted west slowly, working, when he could at various jobs, just whatever he could find. Once he had a small stake put back, he would move on, until he found himself in Willow Springs, and in the company of Bob Sheah. For the last year, he had been in the employment of the Sheah's. It seemed to him like he had found the home he was looking for. He had no intention of leaving, until the day came for him to find a wife and a place of his own and, even then, he knew he wouldn't go far.

The entrance to the trail, leading up to the hanging valley, lay just ahead of the two young men, as they reached the base of the mountain. From here on, it was treacherous travelling, but in a couple hours, they would reach the valley and start making it ready to receive a herd. The trail was narrow with steep walls on one side and a steep drop on the other in some places, but once the cattle were on the trail, they had no choice but to end up at the valley. There was no other outlet to the trail but, even better, there were only a few who knew it was there.

Chapter Thirteen

The train bumped into Kansas City and came to a stop. Gathering his gear, the one-time prize fighter worked his way to the door of the rail car, down the steps, and onto the boardwalk. He had a couple hours here, before the train would leave again and he would be on his way to Denver. His main priority right now was to find a wire office and see if he had a message from Cabel. He had checked at every stop and nothing to this point. It was becoming worrisome, although he carried the actual paperwork on the property, he did not know the lay of the land as Cabel did, and had something happened to Cabel, he wasn't sure he would even be able to find the actual property that he owned. And, if there were issues, he would, for certain, need help solving them. But he knew his brother well and believed in him and his ability. So, up the street he went in search of word from his younger brother.

Kansas City, Missouri was a lot bigger than Dave had anticipated. He felt a little foolish now, seeing all the people here; knowing that as travelled as he considered himself to be, he had never known this many people were here. In his mind, everything out here was desolate and unkempt. What he witnessed, now, was anything but desolate. It was a bustling city, like any other back east, rivalling cities, such as Charleston in size and population. His hopes briefly became high for what it would be like in the Wyoming territory, but that was dashed quickly by seeing the wagons loaded with people coming into town from the west. But, at the same time, he knew what he was looking toward and knew that once he arrived on his own property, he would become happy with the peace and quiet that accompanied it.

The Cabel office was busy as Dave walked in. A lot of the people he recognized from the train, so he assumed it was passengers relaying to family at home they had finished their journey. But it didn't take long for him to get through the line and check if he had a message. He was relieved to find out that he did, however, it disheartened him, somewhat, when he read the message. So, what he had feared was, now, a reality. Squatters had taken the place over and, apparently, weren't going to be happy about leaving, for had it been just a family Cabel could've easily worked that out by himself. But with the message being what it was, Dave, now, knew he was about to walk into a fight. It wasn't really anything new to him, just a new way of fighting, and Dave could only hope he was up to the task.

The train had arrived early in the day, before the sun had really had a chance to show its full capability, but now walking out of the Cabel office, it had come out in full force. The sun blinded him and the heat was stifling. It was hard to believe that in just the few minutes he had been in the office the temperature had changed that much.

He thought about Cabel, out in the wild all these years, with no shelter, other than trees to block the sun. And even now, more than likely, with no place to go to escape the sun and its heat, he would be out trying to figure a way to work through the issues, facing the two of them. Dave could only hope that all was still well with his brother and that they would meet up soon.

With his business attended, Dave made his way back to the train depot and boarded the train. He had a lot to think about, now that he knew there would be trouble, when he arrived. He would have to be quiet about who he was, that was for sure. From this point on, he would have to be careful about whom he talked to and what was said, not just what he said, but every question and every statement made by others toward him, would have to be carefully thought about. He knew no one out here; therefore, he had no one he knew he could trust.

The passenger car was starting to fill up now, as the time drew closer to departure. From here, he started the journey to Denver. There would be few stops, along the route. The stops would be merely to resupply with provisions and water and coal for the boilers. Dave's attitude had changed completely now, from one of wonder and amazement at what he was doing and all he knew he would see, to one of distrust and caution of anyone and everyone he came in contact with. He, now, looked at the gentleman making his way down the aisle and wondered if he was part of a gang that may try to kill him. And the young lady sitting across from him; was she trying to make casual conversation or secretly grilling him for information? This was not the way he had intended to start his new life out west, but whatever it is, is what it will be. Let come what may, he would be up to the task.

The time passed slowly, he tried to sleep, but it was difficult. Between the noise made by the rails and now the dreams of what was to come, he slept only fitfully, waking regularly. It seemed like forever had passed by the time the train rolled slowly into Denver. This would be the last stop for him to enjoy the comforts, if that is what it could be called, of travelling aboard the train. From here on, it would be by wagon, at least to Steamboat Springs where he would purchase a horse and gear and set out into the territory. As Dave stood up to leave his seat, he remembered a part of the message that Cabel had sent him, "Come quiet and Come heeled," so with that in mind, he reached in his bag and pulled out his revolver. He had rarely carried it over the years, for most of where he went he had plenty of people around him that knew better how to handle them. But, now, he felt a little vulnerable for maybe the first time in his life, so sticking the colt in the front of his belt, he made his way off of the train and out onto the boardwalk toward the livery. He hoped to find a group headed out in the next couple of days, especially, since he knew Cabel was in trouble, but that would be extremely lucky.

Denver, like Kansas City, was considerably larger and more advanced than he had expected. Asking for directions to the livery, he discovered there were several to choose from and once finding out where the closest one was, he headed that way, crossing busy streets, passing restaurants, saloons and hotels, along the way. Dave could not believe how many people had already made their way out west. And judging from the buildings, some had been here for generations.

Finally, rounding a corner, the livery came in view, and after a brief conversation with the tender, learned that he would be able to secure passage to Steamboat on a stage, leaving the very next day. This worked out well, as the note sent to him by Cabel was still weighing on his mind. He knew his brother could take care of himself but still hated the thought that he might be in trouble with no help to be found. And that it would also mean that he would lose his partner. And, to make it worse, the partner that knew about the business they were getting into. Dave knew nothing much at all about cattle or land. Fighting, however, now that was a subject he knew.

After a good meal, Dave made his way to the hotel nearest the livery where he would board the stage the next morning and procured a room for the night. His mind raced, as he thought of the adventure that lay ahead of him. Never before had he been this far west and already marveled at the scenery he had been missing out on for so long. But, in his mind, was worry as well. Was his brother still in trouble? Was he even still alive? Could he find him, once he arrived? There were no good directions to where he was going, only faint 'follow this trail' type. There were no major roads to go by, only pig trails. No road signs, only mountains and certain landmarks to follow. It was an exciting time for Dave Glaize, but also a time full of anxiety. And this being his last night in anything that resembled civilization, only heightened that anxiety and, in turn, kept him awake on a night that he knew he should rest.

A slight tap on the door woke him, before he had even known he had fallen asleep. With the voice of the night man telling him it was time to get up. So, this was it. He was really heading out to the wild. It almost seemed surreal, as he gathered his gear, made his way to the stables, and boarded the stage headed to a town that wasn't really even a town. Only a few people even lived in Steamboat and the name hadn't even been made official. It did have a few of the necessary amenities but nothing really to speak of. Nevertheless, he was on his way, and from there on to Willow Springs by horse back. Another town that went only by its nickname, these were towns that may not even survive more than a few years. That's where he was going.

Chapter Fourteen

Albert Hitchens had been around this country only a few years, but was known by most everyone as an honest, but hard man. He had a no non-sense way about him that caused lesser men to think of him as someone to be feared, because he wasn't quick with a smile. As a matter of fact, he hardly ever smiled at all. But, to his family, he was a wonderful man with a big heart. And although he didn't smile, they knew his gruff, hard edge that was present, when he was working was gone away when around his family. To the men that he dealt with, they knew he was someone to be feared, for he was a fierce adversary when pushed and it didn't take a lot of pushing to find the ugly side of Albert Hitchens. He and his family had fought drought, starvation, Indians, and all the other hardship, when making their way out west and more since arriving, but he had pulled them through by sheer will, at times, it seemed. Now, most of that was past him and he was a shrewd businessman in a business where shrewdness was a must. And even though his age was starting to show, he was still as strong as most anyone and could work alongside the best. To the men, who worked for him, he was hard but fair. He treated everyone with the utmost respect, when it was deserved, but would not hesitate to handle business, when that respect was lost. It was primarily for this reason that the men that worked for him were known as some of the best cowhands in the country and the same reason that, to a man, they would not hesitate to fight or die for him. And there was no doubt in any of them that he would do the same.

Once you had worked for Albert Hitchens, as long as you left on good terms, for he never faulted a man for leaving and trying to better himself, you were a friend for life. And this was what Cabel was hoping for, as he rode in to Poole and into the Hitchen's ranch.

The place hadn't changed much in the couple years, since Cabel had last seen it. The small-town set in a semi-circle around the small pool of water, for which the town was named. To the south of the town, was the ranch house, and the town was pretty much encircled by the ranch. Albert had moved in and settled, then over time others had moved in, some staying on and others heading out after time. A lot of the ones that left found that the country was considerably more rugged and cold than they imagined. This is how Albert was able to gain so much property, a lot of those that had left sold their property to Mr. Hitchens, in order to finance the trip back home. There were not a lot of fences, due to the size of the place and the number of hands he was able to employ. Plus, just the way the land was formed helped keep the cattle on the Hitchens range. Down by the house, were the barn and corrals that you would find on any ranch at the time. North of the town was a draw that was used a lot as a corral. It had sides that went up in a steep 'V' shape and a sheer wall at the north end. Once in this draw, there was only one way back out.

Albert Hitchens was leaning against one of the corrals, watching one of his hands attempt to break one of the many mustangs that freely roamed the area, as Cabel rode up.

"These boys are gonna learn about catching these older stud mustangs. They get their butts kicked every time. Anything over about four years old is just too much trouble, especially a stud horse. Now, we are going be here all day, watching these men get thrown all over Colorado," Albert Hitchens stated shaking his head, but without turning around to see who he was talking to.

"You want me to take a turn at him, Boss?" Cabel said in return, smiling at the fact that some conversations never change, the participants do, but the content doesn't.

"No, Cabel, I appreciate it, but you would probably just hurt yourself, and seeing as how you don't work for me anymore, I might feel bad about that. Well, on second thought, naa, I probably wouldn't either," he laughed as he turned around, "How you been, boy? Long time no see."

Cabel dismounted and the two men shook hands like old friends. After exchanging pleasantries, it was time to get down to business.

"You need what?" Albert exclaimed, "You mean to tell me you went and bought three hundred head of cattle with no one to get them home for you? Boy, I thought you were smarter than that."

"Well, you see, Mr. Hitchens, I am kind of forced to make some drastic moves at this point. As soon as I am able to get my place, I have to be ready to move. I figured there would still be some folks hanging around, but it seems as though they've all gone for the season. But if you can't afford to lose a few guys for a week or so, I understand. I can handle the cattle myself, it's just that I wanted to ride on up north and scout the trail and the destination."

"Up north, you say? I have heard there was getting ready to be some trouble up north of here, around Willow Springs, something to do with the Brantley place, that wouldn't be you would it?"

"Yes, sir, I'm afraid it would. And I am in the right. Every claim I have on the place will hold up in a court of law. And I would wager he has nothing that can match it."

Albert thought about it a minute, then looked back at Cabel, "You ain't expecting me to pay the wages, too, are you? Cause if you are, you're out of luck."

"No, sir, I will pay each man a month's wages, whether it takes a month or a few days. But they have to fend for themselves on grub and what not. I don't have no chow wagon or cook to send with them."

"Well, I really don't care too much for that damned Cobb Brantley, anyway. It will be good to have a neighbor I like, even if only a little bit. Yea, I'll go check and see who wants to go. Shouldn't need more than four, I guess."

"Thank you very much, Mr. Hitchens, I owe you one. If you would, just have them meet me at the restaurant in town in the morning about seven. I will give them instructions from there. Oh, tell them they should be back in a week or so. I've got to head back to Steamboat and take care of some business, thank you again, Mr. Hitchens."

The ride back to Steamboat was pleasant. Not just that the weather was nice, but his plan was starting to come together now. His cattle would be headed north in a couple days, with him riding ahead and scouting the trail. Dave would be here, at any time, and headed to Willow Springs and if he had received the message, he would be acting like any other newcomer to the town. They would meet up, after the cattle was safe, in the hanging valley. He had to remind himself from time to time that it was not a done deal yet, although things were going good, this thing was a long way from being over.

Cabel slept that night but not very well. All of his enthusiasm from the ride back from Poole had slowly slipped away and he was back to reality, by the time he arrived at his hotel in Steamboat. His thoughts had turned to the players; in what was happening to him. Most of them, he had figured out alright, but there was still a few he wasn't too sure about; Mose Dellinger, being one of them. Where did he fit in in the grand scheme of things? Was he involved with the Brantleys? Cabel felt sure that he was and that he would have to contend with him as well, before all was over. He was surely not going to just go away because he was asked to by the true landowner. It would cost him too much money. But would he be willing to fight for it? And if he was, how many men would he have to throw in with the Brantleys?

Cabel was up, before the sunlight stared through the window. He had a big day ahead of him, a big next couple weeks actually, now that he thought about it. So, sliding on his boots and hitching up his gun-belt, he made his way down the stairs and across the street to meet with the boys from the Hitchens ranch.

The restaurant was fairly crowded this time of the morning, for these were hardworking people, so they were up early any way. Add on top of that, winter was coming and there was a lot to do, before the snow started. Off in one corner, he spotted the men he was looking for, three weathered looking cowboys who looked like they could handle whatever needed be, so he made his way over and introduced himself.

Using his finger on the table, he drew out an invisible map, explaining the approximate location of the hanging valley, while explaining that he had never been there personally. He also explained that he was going to ride ahead and try to head off any trouble, before they got there and that they should send a rider to the Sheahs, if he hadn't joined them before they reached the entrance to the valley.

He thought briefly about whether or not he could trust these men, but if they were sent by Albert Hitchens, they were good men, for that's the only way he would have kept them around. So, with this being settled and after laying out the plan to them, he took out. They were to get the herd ready to move and out of town today, as quietly as they could. The fewer that knew they were working for him, the better. Once out of town at a safe distance, they were to hold up for another full day before heading north, giving Cabel time to get ahead and, hopefully, remove any trouble. Cabel needed this drive to go smooth as possible.

Once back outside, he went to the Last Chance, looking for Jack Nelson. With him not being there, he headed to the corrals, surely, he would be there and he was right.

"Hello, Mr. Glaize. Right on time, we were just cutting your three hundred head out. Care to join us?"

"Well, not trying to be rude, Mr. Nelson, but no, sir. I wouldn't. I trust you will give me what I pay you for. Plus, I need to go ahead and get on the trail. There is all kind of trouble that this herd could run into, before it gets where it is headed and I am hoping to take care of some of it, before it happens. I have some boys that will be along, shortly, to pick them up and start heading them out of town. But I do have your money and if you don't mind, we can settle up."

"Fair enough, I guess," Jack said, "Just a warning to you though, son, those Brantleys will go through hell, before you take that place from them."

This was not something that Cabel was not aware of, but he listened like he had never heard it. Often times, a man can be told the same thing more than once and get a little more information out of it each time. And this time was no different, for he found out that, *yes*, Mose Dellinger did have his hand in the Brantley ranch, and that, *yes*, he would fight to keep it. But the question still remained how much help he had to give. He had seen no one in town that looked the part, so they would either be outside of town, at the Brantleys, maybe, or had headed south for the w…the thought came to him, suddenly. He had been planning to wait, until spring, to finalize this thing but, now, he was thinking he should only wait, until it got cold; downright bitter cold, the kind that goes all the way to the bone.

"Well, good luck to you, son, I sincerely wish you the best," Jack stated, as the two men shook hands. And with the money paid and the cattle being rounded up, it was time for Cabel to head back up north. It had been nice around here for the last couple days with no trouble, but that wouldn't last much longer, for he knew, once he got out away from people, any number of things were bound to happen.

Riding past the stables, on his way out of town, he noticed the stage was coming in; that made him wonder how much longer, before Dave arrived. He didn't even stop to think that Dave may have been on that one. And he was.

Chapter Fifteen

Taking an easterly route out of town, Cabel had plans to circle back around to the north and west, once he was well out of sight. He was sure any enemies would know he was headed back toward Willow Springs, but he wanted to make them work, as much as he could to track him. He had no plans of heading back the way he had taken when he came to Steamboat, but it would have to be close and, at least, one pass that he would have to travel was the same. This worried him, for his enemies knew this as well, and he had made more enemies in town, and sure didn't do much to repair relations with the enemies he already had. But that is how it goes, sometimes, when you stand for what you believe in. Cabel had always had a way of rubbing folks the wrong way, even if he wasn't trying. He had never had the friendly, jovial manner that some had, his was always gruff and hard edged and, in turn, misunderstood more times than not.

The trail climbed steadily, as he turned more north than west. As the terrain continued to rise, the difference in temperature could be obviously felt. Cabel knew a little about this part of the country, therefore, knew what the winters were like. It was not going to be fun to be out and around in another month. His only hope was that he could get his cattle up into the hanging valley, before the trail got too bad. Right now, from what he had learned from Bob Sheah, it was going to be tough going, as it was, once it started snowing, it sounded as if it would be next to impossible. But, one thing at a time, first the cattle had to get there. Then worry about climbing the trail in. Of course, this brought on further questions like feed and water all winter. Not just for the cattle, but for himself, for someone had to stay with the cattle. Shelter was going to be another issue, for he would not be able to just open his bed roll under the stars in forty below weather with a blowing snow.

Continuing north, Cabel knew he was well to the east of the route he had taken on his way down, so he continued on. Once he topped the mountain, he would turn more to the west, crossing his original path, and skirt the path about a mile to the west. The cattle would have to go another way, for there was no way to get a herd of cattle through here. The climbing had become more and more steep, as the miles wore on, and at times, Cabel had to dismount and lead the dun through the worst of it. The shale rock was apt to slide at any time, sending horse and man on an uncontrolled tumble back down the mountain.

Stopping for a breather, Cabel had the opportunity to turn and look at the way he had come. From his vantage point, he could see just how beautiful the valley was. The Yampa River ran through the bottom of the valley, just to the south of where the towns were starting to pop up. A few miles to the west, another town was starting to spring up and then further on was another one. *"It was sad,"*

Cabel thought to himself; that one day this whole valley would be full of houses and people.

Mounting back up, he continued on north. He was almost to the top and feared it would be even colder on the north side of the mountain. He would have to be on the lookout now, for somewhere to camp tonight that would be out of the wind, for on this side, the north wind would surely have a bite to it. And finding something close to what he was looking, he made camp for the night. He knew that tomorrow could bring any number of challenges and that is aside from the fact that, tomorrow, he would have to meet back up with his original path and make it through the pass with no trouble. He had a hunch someone would be waiting for him, as he went through there, and there was lots of places for a man to hide, if he wanted to dry gulch another man.

Daylight broke and found him already in the saddle. He had turned, now, back toward the east, to meet up with his previous trail and start into the pass. Pulling out his canteen, he rinsed his mouth and allowed a drink of water. His mouth was dry, partly from the dry air, and partly from knowing the possibility of what could happen shortly. But, after a short break, he made his way onto the main trail, and after stopping to assess, made his way into the pass.

The pass was narrow here, with wall that angled steeply up about three hundred feet. Here, he was fairly safe, for the hiding places hadn't shown themselves yet. Further on through the pass, the bottom opened up to about a hundred feet wide and the sides, although just as high, were not as steep. Great boulders had fallen over time and had stopped at various places, along the slope, allowing for places a man could wait on a passerby, for whatever intentions he had. Cabel knew what the intentions would be if someone were waiting on him in one of these places, so his eyes were constantly moving, alert for anything. The flicker of an ear on a deer, a bird suddenly flew up in the path in front of him, the porcupine waddling his way up the bank looking for a place in the rock, in which, to hide, all these things he noticed but nothing out of place. He notice the cave on the west side, about one hundred feet up from the floor of the pass, and wondered how many animals had used that cave for shelter, over the years. How many men had possibly used it for shelter during storms? The entrance was partially hidden by scrub oaks and he hadn't noticed it on the way south. That, too, would be a good place for someone to hide from their prey, if they were of a mind to, but no movement, no flashes from sunlight gleaming off of a rifle barrel, no rocks rattling down the slope where a man had slid or kicked them trying for a better position, all seemed quiet.

The sides slowly started to slope more and more, as he neared the end of the pass, soon, he would turn back to the east and get away from his previous route and it could not happen sooner. He had grown accustom to taking a different route every time, when at all possible, for in this country, it was easy for a man to make enemies. And even if he hadn't, there was no law, so men did as they pleased. And while most of those were good men, there were a lot who weren't. These were the ones that would hold up in a pass, such as the one he just came through and shoot anyone passing through, just to see what they had. He had heard of people getting killed, for no more than a few dollars or a watch of little value, just because the killer thought the traveler may have something of value.

Fully clear of the pass, now, Cabel made a quick turn to his right and started moving to the east. The trees were getting thicker and a little taller now, as he continued making his way back down the mountain. Baggs would be just to his north and west, he would skirt around it, for there would surely be trouble there, and make his way on up toward Willow Springs, then turn east and north again, toward the entrance to the hanging valley. It would be good to get there and, even better, once he knew the herd was safe in the valley.

Suddenly, his horse stumbled, and in the instant, before he heard the report of the rifle, he tried to figure why. Then just as he heard the rifle, he felt a tug on his shirt, down low, just above his hip, and then he heard the rifle again. *"This was not good,"* he thought to himself, as he kicked himself free of the falling horse. Someone had thought well enough to know that he would be extra cautious, coming through the pass, so they decided to wait until he was through and not as on edge. They must have guessed which way he would turn leaving the pass or, maybe, they had men in both directions. All these things passed through his mind, as he fell. And as he watched the dun's legs crumble from under him, he was down, too.

Cabel had managed to kick himself free of the horse on the way down, so he wasn't trapped, that was a good thing at least, but his horse had landed on his rifle, which was still in its boot on the side of the saddle, so it was of no use. Then he heard voices, they were coming to make sure they had accomplished their mission. And one of the voices he recognized, for sure. It was Tough Brantley.

"Are you sure you hit him?" Tough said quietly, as they two men eased their way through the brush in search of their prey, who they knew was down.

"Oh yea, Tough, he's hit and hard. I could tell by the sound. That thud tells me gut shot. He'll still be alive, but probably not for much longer. Plus, even if he ain't gut-shot, he's hurt bad, and with no horse, he will never get out of here alive. This is bad country for snow. I say we leave him be, he'll die soon enough."

Cabel recognized the voice of the other man, but couldn't place who it was, but what he said, worried him. He hadn't had time to assess his wound, yet, to know how bad he was hit, but he knew the man was right about one thing, he was hit hard.

For a while, after the voices faded away, he continued to lay still, the pain was terrible, and fear had gripped him in a way he had never known before. He had to think, plan, anything to occupy his mind, so he would be able to do the things necessary for his survival. He crawled on his belly, over to where his horse had fallen and checked for any supplies that he could get to. He found his canteen, and a little bit of jerky that had been in his saddle bags. There was a box of .44 cartridges as well, so he grabbed them, along with the other items and his bed roll and then he rolled over to his back to assess his situation. He was hit hard and down low, if he was gut-shot, he didn't know, but he would have to wait to find out. The wind was picking up now and it had a bite to it. Looking at the clouds that were forming overhead, it just might be the first snow of the year. It could've come at a better time.

Shelter, at this point, was his first concern and the trees, he was in, offered very little. He thought of the cave he noticed back in the canyon, could he make it there? He would have to try, it was his only choice. Crawling to the nearest tree, he managed to get to his feet. The pain in his right side was excruciating, as he tried to walk, but he forced himself to continue forward. He must be a quarter mile or so from the entrance to the pass then, if his memory was true, another couple hundred yards, and then the climb up to the cave. This would prove to be the hardest thing he had ever tried to do, but it was the only way he could see himself surviving.

Once out of the trees and with nothing to hold on to, he stumbled and fell several times before making it to the bottom of the slope where the cave should be. This should actually be easier, he thought to himself knowing that from here on, for it would be easier for him to crawl up the slope. Hand over hand and using his one good leg, he worked his way up the slope. Finally, the scrub oak that guarded the entrance came into his view and he felt that just beyond that was safety. At least, temporarily.

Pulling his knife, just in case, he slid his way around the guard and peered into the cave. It was bigger that he had thought, a man could almost stand up in the mouth, and it appeared to go into the mountain, a couple hundred feet. This wasn't going to be too bad after all.

Pulling himself on further into the cave, he was looking around. Someone has used this same cave before, for there was dry firewood stacked neatly against the wall and he could see the markings where the fire had been, but it looked to be a long time ago. Slipping his knife back in is sheath, he crawled in still further, and rolling over to back, against the wall, looked down to take the first look at the wound.

The growl came from deeper in the cave and Cabel froze. Fear knotted up inside him, as he heard it and knew, at once, he was in trouble. The mountain lion must have had the same idea he had and, now, he was in its way of safety, which meant it was cornered. He looked down at his revolver, with the thong over the hammer, so he wouldn't lose it, while trying to crawl; there was no way he could get it in time. And, at his knife, tucked neatly in its sheath, only thirty seconds ago it was in his hand and, now, it may as well be lying in the trees with his horse. Knowing he had no other choice, he reached for it, and at that moment, the cougar pounced.

Chapter Sixteen

Dave's knees seemed, at first, like they would not hold him up, as he stepped down from the stage. The long ride in the cramped area had taken its toll and it would be a while before he was able to feel normal again. He desperately wanted a hot meal and a good night's rest, but the message from Cabel was weighing on him, so he turned immediately toward the stock pens, in search of a horse.

A tall slender man in a black hat was the first to greet him, when he walked up.

"There something I can help you with, son?"

"Yes, sir, there is. I just got off the stage and need a good horse. Is that something you can help with?"

"Yep, that would be so. What did you say your name was? You look awful familiar," Jack was no tenderfoot, he knew exactly who he was talking to, at least, he thought he did.

Dave, remembering what the message had said, was hesitant to answer the question. Who was this man and was he friend or foe? Did he know Cabel, for there was a strong family resemblance between him and his brother that could easily be recognized? The man had a friendly way about him, but then again, most evil men did, when they needed to, so that couldn't be counted on.

"Mr. Nelson, we've got Cabel's cattle bunched up and ready to move. Is everything good?"

It was a young cowhand that had walked over from the main corral, where a fair amount of cattle were being held in preparation to be moved.

"Yea, we're good, here let me get you the bill of sale, I wouldn't want you to get caught by the wrong person with all these different brands," Jack stated, as he reached into his book for the paperwork, "Barrett, this is Mr.," Then he turned toward Dave, "I'm sorry, sir, what did you say your name was again?"

Dave's mind was racing now, for Cabel wasn't a name that was common anywhere, much less out here. They had to be talking about his brother. These must be his cattle, for Cabel had told him of his plan to buy cattle, as soon as possible to get things going. If these men were moving Cabel's cattle that must mean that he trusted them.

Smiling a little now, Dave responded, "Well, I didn't say, but I am Dave Glaize. I am Cabel's brother. It's good to meet you."

"Yea, that's what I thought you would say. You boys look a lot alike. Be careful though, your brother has made some enemies. He's made friends, too, don't get me wrong, but some pretty formidable enemies," Jack said with a serious look in his eyes, "Dave, this is Barrett Cross, he works for the Hitchens ranch, over west of here a piece, but has hired on to move Cabel's, well, your cattle, too, I guess, on up back up the country. Barrett, I assume he gave you instructions on where you're going?"

"Yes, sir, as well as he could. I know that country pretty good up in that area, so we shouldn't have too much trouble, as long as we are left alone, anyway. Dave, you're more than welcome to travel along with us if, you're of a mind to."

"Well, I would really like to meet up with Cabel as soon as possible and see how things are going. Is he still in town?"

"No, I don't think so, I saw him headed east, about twenty minutes ago. I figure he'll ride east a while, then turn back north, and west, there's only one good pass to get through, without going way out of the way. Now, these cattle will have to take the long route, but I figure Cabel will cut straight through."

Barrett Cross squatted and down and using a stick, drew the route that he figured Cabel would have taken and where the pass was located that he would have to get through. And then he repeated the instructions Cabel had given him, as far as where he was to take the cattle, "Now, here is the route we will take with the cattle to get across the mountain. We will hold up here for a day," pointing the stick in the sand, at a point just west and north of Steamboat, "Before we actually get started. Our trail and his should meet up about right in here, which is about twelve or fifteen miles from Willow Springs and about thirty miles from where he said we were headed. We should be at the meet up in about four days. But if you run into any trouble, you have our route. Make your way to us."

With that said and the pleasantries over, Dave proceeded with the business at hand. He purchased two horses from Jack Nelson and headed to the general store. There, he bought a full set up for himself including saddle, saddle bags, and bed roll. And he bought a pack saddle and supplies he figured he would need for the ride north. He figured he was two hours or so behind Cabel, by the time he was all packed up and ready to go. And, so he rode out. This was the furthest west he had been and this type of living was fairly new to him, but he was a good listener and a fast learner. And Cabel had talked a lot, before he left, about what he would need and how things would be. Right now, it just felt good to be out in the fresh air. He was already starting to see the allure of it all and why Cabel loved it so.

Dave rode almost straight north out of town, while Cabel had gone, originally, east. He knew Cabel had done it, for he was a wily young man and knew that someone would be waiting on him to leave and see which way he went. But, it worked well for Dave, because he was hoping to make up some time on Cabel and maybe, come up on him on the trail. Not only would it be good to see his brother again, but with trouble coming, it would be good for them both to have some help.

The trail was steep and, from time to time, he got down walking his horse and taking a good look around. He found a spot where the trail was crossed by another rider and wondered if or even hoped that would be Cabel. Continuing on, he could feel the ground starting to flatten out a little and he could see the mouth of the pass starting to open up in front of him. It was still a long way off, as out here, things were always further away than they appeared and it was starting to get later in the day. To make it worse, he could see the clouds starting to form to the north, just on the other side of the mountain. So, taking shade under a patch of scrub oak, he made a makeshift camp to rest his horse and his body some, before continuing on.

The storm worried him, if it was snow, he had no shelter and the trail was about to get even worse. The good thing was, this time of year it wouldn't stay long, but it would make for miserable and dangerous travel, while it lingered. But he needed to keep moving, if he was going to catch up with Cabel, so after just a few minutes, he dug a piece of jerky out of his bag and continued on.

Once he entered the pass, he could not help but think how easy it would be for someone to hide behind the rocks or trees on either side of the cliff and attack without warning. He thought of Cabel, how many times had he passed through such places and worried, if his enemies were waiting for him? And especially now, knowing his enemies would know he had to travel this way to get back. He noticed, on the hill, to his left, the cave, about one hundred feet up the slope. *"A man could easily get to that cave,"* he thought, then that he would like to explore such places as that. How many men or animals had used that cave, from time to time, as shelter from the elements? He continued riding north.

He had noticed that, just before entering the pass, a set of tracks that joined the trail from the west. He wondered again, if it may have been his brother. It felt exhilarating to know that after all these years of wondering what it was like to move around like Cabel did; that, now, he could be literally following in his steps. He and his brother, although so many miles apart, had always been close, and now it was like a dream come true that they would be living and working together for the rest of their lives. He had idolized Cabel in a way, even though he was the older brother. Cabel had been wild and free, traveling, as he wanted, seeing things that most folks back east weren't aware existed. He had fought with and against Indians, outlaws, wild animals, and even wild elements and had come through. His scars told stories that would amount to dreams in normal people. And, now, he was out there fighting again, but this time, for a new beginning. Not used to looking for such things, Dave had not noticed the faint blood trail and drag marks left by his brother, as he fought for his life literally, instead of figuratively. There was still a good trail, although most of the blood had soaked into the earth.

The snow started falling, as Dave cleared the north end of the pass, light, at first, but getting heavier by the second. While, at first, it was actually exciting to be riding through the storm, reality set in and Dave realized he was going to need shelter and soon. Looking around, he found nothing but sage brush and scrub oaks, none, of which, offered enough shelter. Then he thought of the cave and wondered whether or not it would be deep enough to afford to cover for him and a fire for warmth. Sitting his horse, under a scrub oak limb, he contemplated on whether he should go on or turn around and go back to the cave. He knew he would not get his horses up the slope, so he would have to leave them outside, and looking around, he found a place he could picket them, out of sight of the trail, with, at least, a little grass. The decision was made then; he would go to the cave and see if it would work for temporary shelter.

He was halfway up the slope, before he saw the drop of blood on the rock. He froze with fear, when he noticed it, for he knew that there was either a man or beast hurt inside of the cave or one was hurt on his way out of the cave. Either way, the options weren't good. Then, he noticed the boot mark in the dirt, half covered in snow, but a boot mark no doubt. Someone had climbed up this slope and was hurt bad, when they did.

Reaching the mouth of the cave, he carefully peered in. He was expecting, at any time, to either feel a bullet or for an animal to attack him, but nothing. Easing in a little further, he called out, but again nothing. Looking to his right, he saw the stack of firewood left by some long-gone traveler that knew, at some point, someone else would need this shelter. Then, once inside the cave, without the outside light in his eyes, he noticed on his left what appeared to be a pile of something, of what, he couldn't tell, until he inched closer. The cat was massive, as big as he had ever seen, it was dead. Under the cat, was a man, badly cut up. Dave could only assume he was dead, for the blood was everywhere. Man, and animal blood mixed together covered the floor of the cave, from this point on further into the cave.

Rolling the cat back, he noticed the knife stuck deep in its ribs, along with several other stab wounds. Then he looked at the man, covered in blood, clothes torn nearly off of him, with deep cuts, and scratches around his chest, neck, and face. *"This man had put up a good fight,"* he thought, as he looked closer; it was at that point his heart sank. It was, then, that he realized who the man was. His own little brother, Cabel Glaize. Sitting back on his heels, all he could think about is after all he had been through, he would die like this, in a cave, alone, in a fight with a mountain lion, right here, as things were about to turn for the better. The two brothers separated for years and, now, with the opportunity to live and work together, as brothers should. As he thought about this he heard a sound, faint and weak, and he realized Cabel was alive, but only barely.

Working as quickly as he could, he took a blanket from his bedroll and covered him against the cold. Taking some of the dry wood from the cave, he made a fire to keep the warmth in the cave as well as possible. Then, he did the only other thing he could think of; he left his brother there, went to his horse, and headed south and west, with hopes of meeting up with the herd and help. But on his way out of the cave, he was confused, for one word had been written in blood on the floor; that word was *'Tough'*.

Chapter Seventeen

Seeing the herd coming up the trail was a welcome sight for Sandy Pearson and Will Kollett. For the past week, they had worked on cutting and stacking hay and building shelters to face the upcoming winter. Now that Cabel and the cattle were back, it meant going back home and eating good grub and sleeping in a bed. But as the herd got closer, they realized something was wrong and after a brief conversation, the mood had changed. The mood was now solemn, as they single filed the cattle up the steep and narrow trail to the hanging valley. Dave had arrived, Barrett had explained, and none too soon. And once they had Cabel tended to, he had asked several questions, before paying the guys and heading off on his own. Where to, no one was sure, but he was almighty upset, even more so, once he found out what the word on the floor had to have meant. For during the process, they had discovered that Cabel had been shot. They had found his dead horse and were able to recover his gear. But, then, Dave had left in a hurry.

It was dusk dark, when Dave rode his horse into the yard at the house that he rightfully owned but had been claimed by the Brantley crew. Several of the Brantley men were still out and around and stared as the stranger, so bravely rode up.

"Hey, Brantley. Can you hear me?" Dave yelled, as he rode right up to the front porch. He carried a double barrel shotgun; borrowed from the Hitchens men that had brought the cattle north. He also had his six-gun, both of Cabel's pistols were tucked in his belt, and his Winchester was in its boot.

"Yea, I hear you, who the hell are you?" Cobb Brantley had opened the front door with his pistol in his hand but staring at the double barrel made him wonder if he could raise it in time. He decided it wasn't worth the try.

"Listen up, and listen good. My name is David Glaize. I am the elder brother of Cabel Glaize or was. He's dead. I've heard about what has been going on here and I'm here to tell you it's over. I have a deed to this place, and all the land that goes with it, that will hold up in any court of law. Now, simply because I don't want any of your stuff left behind, you have five days to gather up and get out. If you decide not to leave, I will be back, and when I come back, I won't be near as nice as I am right now. If you're still here, I will assume you want to fight, and make no mistake, I'll kill every single one of you. I'll burn the house with you in it, if I have to. If you doubt me, then feel free to try. Now, this goes for everyone here, with one exception. Which one of you is Tough Brantley?"

"He's my son and he ain't here. What is so special about him?" Cobb Brantley was furious at this point. Never in his life had he been talked to in this manner and he wasn't liking any of it. But, at this point, it only took a glance to see this man was mad and he meant every word of what he said. That shotgun would go off and it would be over with, if he tried anything at all and everyone else knew it, too.

"Tough Brantley ain't no part of this bargain, he dies. I will get my hands on him and I will watch the life, as it fades out of his eyes for killing my brother."

Having said what he came here to say, Dave backed his horse out of the yard, careful to leave the shotgun pointed at the old man. Once out of range, he turned and rode off. The news of his meeting with the Brantleys had already reached the Sheah's by the time he rode up to the bottom of the trail and into the hanging valley. Day one was over.

Slick Montgomery had healed now and was feeling better. With Cabel out of the area, things had been quiet around town and thankfully so. For that is what had given him time to heal. Now, he was hearing things that didn't set well with him. According to rumor, Cabel was dead, killed by tough Brantley on the trail back from Steamboat. And Cabel's brother, Dave, had arrived and laid down the terms to the Brantley crew. Things were shaping up to get ugly real soon, for if Dave was anything like Cabel, he meant what he said. Riding out to the Sheah ranch now, he thought about all of this. Cobb Brantley would certainly never leave like Dave had spelled out and Tough would more than likely come hunting Dave. But, then again, he may stay in the safety of the ranch and the men that were in his employment.

Riding up to the ranch, he could tell that Bob had already received word on what had happened, and they were making preparations.

"So, I guess you heard?" Slick asked, as he rode up.

"Yea, we heard. Dave is up at the hanging valley now. I have to say, I think that boy means what he says. If Brantley don't move, he'll kill the whole bunch of them or try to."

"Yea, I haven't met him yet, but I kind of had the same feeling. What's your plan?"

Bob stopped and thought for a second before responding, to make sure what he was saying was what he meant to say, "Well, my thoughts are pretty simple, Slick. Cobb Brantley's about wore out his welcome around here. I liked Cabel; he seemed like a good man. I think his brother will probably be the same. I figure when this week is over and he rides down there, I'll go with him. Can't quite speak for the rest of my men; wouldn't ask it of them, but if there of a mind to then, they're welcome to come along, I reckon."

"Yea, I'll be going along as well. These Glaize boys are some good ones. The kind we need around here. I think I will ride up to that hanging valley and meet this feller though, before I make up my mind for certain."

"I'm headed that way myself, ride alongside, if you want, I'll show you where it's at."

With that, the two men mounted up and rode out in the direction of the hanging valley.

The cattle were all in the valley and settled down to eating the fresh green grass that filled the valley. It was easy to see why it was named as such, there were cliffs that rose up a couple hundred feet on each side and standing in the meadow, it looked, as though, it was hanging from the mountains on either side. Across the north end, ran a creek that came from a natural spring somewhere up in the mountain and would run year around. The grass had hardly been touched by more than deer or elk, which were plentiful, but hadn't hurt anything. Sandy and Will had worked hard on cutting and stacking the hay and had enough for the winter stacked in one of the caves on the western said, with poles cut to make a block where the cattle couldn't get to it, until it was time. On the eastern side, there were two more caves, one at the floor level and another a little higher up the side, no more than twenty feet, it was in these that Sandy had made makeshift shelters; that a man could wait out the winter. Dave admired the beauty of the place, as he looked around. One day, Sandy would build up here and it would be a wonderful place to spend a life. Then, feeling satisfied with what had been accomplished for the day, he headed toward the upper cave to make up some supper. Day two was over.

Day three brought cooler weather and the sky was threatening snow. In preparations, the group had cut more firewood and opened up a spot, coming off of the creek, where the water would pool and it was deep enough to hold water enough for a day or two, if, for some reason, it was needed. Bob Sheah and Slick Montgomery had arrived later in the day, no doubt wanting to meet Cabel's brother and the man that had laid down the law to the Brantley crew with no back-up. That, in itself, took guts. There was some talk about who and who wouldn't help, when the time came, and although no help was asked for, it seemed, as though, there would be plenty. As the sun dipped slowly behind the western side of the valley, Dave laid back on his bed roll, propped his head on his saddle for a pillow, and decided that tomorrow he would take a ride down and see if the Brantleys had made an effort to move or if they were digging in. As he drifted off to sleep, the thought occurred to him, day three was over.

Day four started off early. Dave was up, before the sun, saddling his horse, getting ready for a trip to what he hoped would soon be his new home. He had bought and paid for it with the help of Cabel and both had high hopes for starting a new life. Now, here he was, probably about to fight to the death, over something that was rightfully his, with his brother in bad shape, maybe alive, maybe not. When he had left him at the doctor in Baggs, he was told not to expect him to live. They had discussed shortly on taking him back to Steamboat, however, the thought that the shooter had probably followed him, when he left was on their minds, plus, Barrett's sister, Kristin, worked at the doctor's office in Baggs, so they felt better about the level of care. Cabel had lost a tremendous amount of blood between the bullet wound and the cuts made by the mountain lion. The worst part though, would be the infection. The cat, just like any other wild animal, carried a lot of infection causing bacteria, both, in his mouth and claws, and it had done a number on Cabel with both. Needless to say, Dave had fully prepared himself that it would be the last time he ever saw his brother alive.

Footsteps behind, made him turn around, "I believe I'll ride with you, if that's ok."

It was Bob Sheah. He had arrived the day before and seemed curious about Dave from the start but had not had a chance to talk with him.

"Yes, sir, of course, the company will be welcome. But I am just riding down to see what's going on. Hopefully, I won't even be seen," Dave replied. He knew the old man was wanting to size him up and what better way than to spend a day or more, riding.

"Yea, I think that's a pretty good idea myself."

Mounting their horses, they rode out.

They rode several miles, before either man spoke; finally, it was Bob, who broke the silence:

"You know, I remember when I was a kid back in the Tennessee hills, there were mountains some like these that I used to run through all day. There was this one that got real narrow in one spot. I used to take off across that narrow ridge, knowing that if I didn't make it, it was going to hurt bad, if not, kill me. But, for some unknown reason, I just had to try it. The older I got, the more I thought about that ridge and how it pertains to everyday life. And what I have figured out is this; sometimes, in our life, we come across those narrow ridges and we have two choices. We can either turn back or try to cross them, knowing full well that if we don't make it, something bad is going to happen. It all depends on whether or not making it across is worth the chance. We all have our own reasons for crossing these ridges and I guess my question to you is this; is your reason for crossing this ridge worth dying for?"

This caught Dave off guard, but he thought for quite some time before he answered.

"You know, my main reason for coming out here was the opportunity to spend the rest of my life in the peace and quiet and with my brother around. Now, the brother part of that will probably not happen, so I'm not sure I have a reason to be here anymore. But the way I see it is, these men have taken that opportunity away from me and if I don't do something about it, what's to keep them from doing the same to others? I've fought all my life, that's all I've ever known really, but this is probably the first time I have ever fought, as much for others as for myself. So, I guess to answer your question; yes, it's worth dying for, if it comes to that."

After that, neither man talked anymore, except for communication about the business at hand. And on the way back, they discussed what was about to happen in two days.

Riding back into the valley, the questions came. Everyone had guessed where they had gone and Slick had even seen them leave, but figuring the old man wanted to talk to Dave, he didn't offer to go with them. The Brantley bunch was still at the cabin and it appeared, as though, they had not made a move to start leaving, so it was going to happen. Dave had not lost his resolve; he had told the men what he expected and what would happen if they refused to comply; now, it was time to follow through.

He let Bob handle answering the questions and went on up to his cave to think. He had to plan how this was going to happen or, at least, how those that went with him would stay alive. Day four was over.

Chapter Eighteen

Day five started with thick clouds and the first snow of the year. It came down thick and wet and built up fast. By noon, there was a foot of snow throughout the valley. The cattle were able to paw through the snow for most of the morning but if it continued, it would be time to start feeding from the hay that had been put up for the oncoming winter.

Most of the day was spent cleaning weapons and making plans for the probable upcoming fight that would happen tomorrow, if the Brantley's had not abandoned the ranch. All four of the men that had brought the cattle up, had decided to fight along with Dave. Plus, there was Slick, Bob, Sandy, and Will that would join. In total, there were nine of them and the plan was pretty simple, although, none really liked it. Dave would ride in, while the rest held back. Dave had hoped that it would still be handled without gun play, but if not, he didn't want the others directly in the line of fire. This was his fight and while he appreciated the help of the others, he would rather not see them killed for this. This didn't come without argument, of course, for the others exclaimed they weren't fighting for Dave, it was for the good of the valley, but in the end, Dave won out and everyone ended up agreeing that it was a good plan.

The snow broke that afternoon, but because they knew they would be gone tomorrow, they went ahead and spread a part of the hay out for the cattle and made sure the ice was not choking off the water. With this accomplished, they ate a good supper of fresh elk that Sandy had killed and without much talking, turned in for the night. Day five was over.

The air was crisp and cold, as they saddled up and got ready to head out of the valley. The snow from the day before was still on the ground and would make the trail down the mountain even worse than it already was, but it should be passable, and after that, everyone would be riding with caution and loaded weapons. The Brantley's shouldn't know where the hanging valley was or even that that was where they were at, but no one knew for sure. The ride to the ranch would be nothing like the dime store novels made it look. There would be no nine men, riding side by side, at full speed heading to the showdown. This would be nine men, carefully making their way, attention being paid to every step, conscious of every movement, by any creature that stirred. There was nothing about it, romantic, it was, each man riding, thinking his own thoughts; some thinking about the family members that would miss them, others wondering if anyone would; trying desperately to think of someone that might cry, as they were laid in the ground.

For Dave, there was none of these thoughts. His thoughts were of his brother, probably dead, shot down from hiding by these men, or, at least, some of them.

These were bad men and no longer had a comfortable place here and Dave was about to make sure of it.

The sun was high in the sky now and the temperature had warmed considerably, when he noticed something or was it someone in the trail, ahead of them. Getting closer, he could see it was someone and he was wearing a badge. Reaching for his rifle, Dave's hand was caught by Slick, as he rode up next to him.

"That's Marshall Kolb. He'll blow you right out of that saddle."

"Judging by the look of you, you would be Dave Glaize. I wanna see that paperwork that has caused so much trouble."

"What's this got to do with you, Marshall? We ain't in town and none of this is taking place in town," Bob Sheah spoke up.

"Well, it ain't much gonna take place anywhere, I don't think. Most of the Brantley crew lit out yesterday. It seems they didn't mind working for ole Cobb but wasn't ready to die for him. However, I want to make sure this is legal, at least, as far as I can tell, and I want it to stay out of my town. I won't have this thing carrying over."

"Well, no offense, Marshall, but if you want this kept out of town, you need to be in town getting those fellers out of town. The ones that left yesterday, I will leave alone, as long as they steer clear. But as for any that stay and fight, I won't stop until they're gone," Dave said, as he handed the deed, along with the proof of sale, signed by Mr. Williams and notarized as authentic.

After taking a careful look at the paperwork, Marshal Kolb agreed that Dave had a legal claim to the property, and after one last warning to keep the fight outside of town, the men were on their way, once again.

The ranch looked deserted from the tree line, almost a half mile away to the north. There was no movement, other than the few horses milling around in the stable on the east side by the barn. The Marshall had said that most of the crew had lit out but Dave was sure there would still be several of the main players left. He had not formally met any of them, yet, but all had been described to him and the layout of the land and the situation, up to this point, had explained as well. He knew that Cobb Brantley and his son, Tough, would be there, along with the Lawtons and Lucky Parnell, how many others, he didn't know.

Keeping to the trees, most of the group moved to the east, leaving Sandy Pearson where they currently stood to watch for anyone trying to escape and head toward the herd or the home of Bob Sheah. Barrett Cross and one of his men headed off to the west.

As the group circled around to the east, they were able to get closer to the ranch and see a little better.

"That'll be the Lawton boys, hiding there in the barn," Bob said, as they studied the situation. The two men, one upstairs looking out of the door to the loft and the other, looking through the window on the bottom, appeared to be on sentry duty, "I'm surprised they're still here, I wouldn't have figured they would have hung around. They aren't bad boys; they just fell in with the wrong bunch," Then after studying the situation for a bit, he added, "I, sure, would like to get into that barn. From there, you could get to the house with no one seeing, I believe."

"Yea, I was just thinking the same thing. I tell you what, I don't think they have seen us yet, if y'all will continue on around past the house and fire off a couple shots, I believe these boys here will adjust their position and if so, I can sneak up this little stand of trees and be in the barn, before they know what's up. What you think, Bob?" Dave had been considering ways he could get to the barn, without alerting anyone as well. There was really only one person, here, he wanted to kill and it was neither of the Lawton's. If he could get in the barn, without being seen, he may be able to talk those boys into leaving peacefully.

"Sounds like a plan. We'll go around to the other side of the house but where these boys will still be able to see what's happening, then fire a few shots and hunker down."

Dave had carefully worked his way through the small stand of trees, leading toward the barn by the time the shooting started, to a point no more than thirty yards from the barn, and just as he had thought, the two sentries were now focused on the point to the west, where the shooting had come, allowing him a few seconds to cross the opening and reach the corner of the barn.

Easing around the east side, he peered in the window. The one man was on the other side, looking west, while the other was still up in the loft. If he could get in this side and slip up behind the one on the ground, without being seen by either, he just may have a chance.

Slipping along the east side of the barn and turning the corner, he was more exposed but there was a door here and cracking it open he looked in, all was still clear. The boys were so focused to the west and so secure in their position, they never noticed the man slipping in the door and, now, within five feet of the man on the ground floor.

"You see 'em Tommy?" the one in the loft yelled down to his brother.

"No, I can't see nothing. They're there, though."

The gun barrel in his ribs made Tommy Lawton freeze in his tracks, and after slowly turning around, he knew he was in serious trouble. The eyes that he looked into were cold and mad. He didn't know the man, but knew in a glance who he must be.

"Now, you just drop those guns and keep your mouth shut and you'll live through this, one word and it's all over for you. Here's how this is gonna play out. You're gonna tell your brother, up there, to drop his guns and come on down. I'm not here to kill either of you boys, but be assured I will," Dave said quietly, as Tommy lowered his rifle and gun belt to the ground. There was no anger or hatred in his eyes, only fear. It was one of those times in life that make you question where you are in life as compared to where you want to be.

"Hey, Frank," Tommy yelled up to his brother, "Do me a favor, put your rifle and your gun belt down right where you are and come down the ladder nice and slow. This guy is fixing to blow me in half with this scatter gun, if you don't."

"Do as he says, Frank, and both of you ride out of here safe and sound. Get stupid and Tommy, here, is a dead man. You may get me, before I get you and you may not, what's it worth to you?"

The shooting had quietened down now and Dave was able to hear Frank mumble, as he laid down his weapons and worked his way down the ladder from the loft.

"Easy, mister, we didn't really want to be in this fight anyway. We were just figuring on making some wages to hole up for the winter. If you let us go, I can promise you that you'll never see either of us again."

"Alright then, get on your horses and ride out to the east. Keep the barn between you and the house, so no one sees you leave. If I see you around again, I am going to assume you came back to continue the fight and will treat you as such."

"Yes, sir, and thank you. You'll not see either of us again. Come on, Tommy, I think Texas sounds pretty good about right now."

With the Lawton boys gone, that only left the men in the ranch house and judging by the amount of gun fire earlier, there wouldn't be more three or four in there, so, now, Dave sat for a minute and thought about how he should tackle the house. He thought about how Cabel might do things, but yet, at the same time, he was not Cabel and not only did he have his own way of doing things, he was not as experienced at these types of problems. His thoughts went to his brother and the question of whether or not he was alive. He doubted that he was, for Cabel was in bad shape, when he left him in Baggs. Kristin Cross had taken one look at Cabel and the look in her eyes told Dave all he needed to know and that was that his first instinct was right. Dave figured that, by now, for sure, Cabel had died and that it would be up to him to bury his brother, when this was over. But this had to be done. His brother had fought and now, probably, died for it. So, now, it was time to move, to finish it. He made up his mind, then, that surprise was his best bet, for speed was not on his side.

Slipping out of the front door of the barn now and heading in the direction of the house, his intent was to be seen by his own men and, thus, use the same technique as before. However, being so far away, he was not sure if they would be able to recognize him or not. Surely, they had seen the Lawton boys leaving out and would know that it was him, but he had no way of telling or if they had figured out what he wanted, until the shooting started or until it didn't.

Carefully, he made his way across the small yard to the front porch. He could hear the conversations going on inside, as the men discussed what each opinion was about what was going on. There was one that didn't like the situation at all and felt they should go through the front door and work their way around to the men, waiting in the woods. Another questioned how many were out there.

As he stood at the door, the shots came again from the tree line. So, they had seen him then and guessed what he wanted them to do. Almost as fast as the shots started from the trees, he could hear cursing and firing from inside the ranch house, one more time he went through it in his mind, the first to turn caught the shotgun, then he wouldn't worry about reloading, he would throw it down and pull his six-guns, one from its holster and the other from his waistband and from there, there was no plan. Taking a breath, he went through the front door.

The first to turn was Lucky Parnell, the shotgun blast caught him square in the chest, and he was dead before he hit the ground. *"Something was wrong,"* he thought to himself, as he turned to face Cobb Brantley, *"There weren't enough men in this room,"* he was thinking, as he pulled the trigger, only to hear the sickening sound of the hammer falling on an empty chamber. He must've pulled both triggers the first time on Lucky. All these thoughts were coming to him in flashes, as he dove to his left to avoid the stab of flame coming from Cobb Brantleys pistol. He felt the bullet whiz past his head, as he fired two quick rounds into the old man, sending him slumping to the floor.

Yelling from behind him, made him turn on his backside to see a door open from another room and he fired, as he saw a man coming through the door. That was Tough, according to the description, he was given by Bob Sheah, but there was one more man in the room that was briefly blocked by Tough, as he fell to the ground still holding on to his pistol. The last man dropped his rifle and threw up his arms.

Rising to his feet, he walked over to Tough Brantley, still alive but not by much. His breathing was shallow and hoarse and blood came in bubbles from his mouth, as he tried harder and harder to keep breathing.

"I told the old man I would watch you die, for what you did to my brother, now, here, we are just, as I said," he said, as he looked into the pleading, dying eyes of Tough Brantley.

Then in a barely audible voice, through the blood Tough replied, "I didn't shoot him, it was…"

And, he died.

"Ok, now, who are you?" Dave turned his attention to the one man left standing. Still standing with his arms raised in the air.

"Mose Dellinger. I was just caught up in this, I came out here to discuss business and had no idea this was going on. I swear it. Had I known this, I would've never come out here. I am not a fighter, just a businessman," Mose said, as he slowly lowered his hands to his sides.

"For someone who says they ain't no fighter, you sure carry that sidearm well, Mr. Dellinger. How about you unbuckle that belt real slow and pitch it over here," Dave demanded, as he heard the front door open and Bob Sheah burst in the room.

"Damn, boy, for an easterner, that don't know how to handle a gun, you sure can make a mess," Bob looked around the room in amazement.

"Who said I didn't know how to handle a gun? I've been shooting all my life, same as Cabel," Dave replied with a grin, "I'm better at fighting with my hands though, more fun."

Then, focusing his attention back to Mose, he said, "What kind of business you doing with this rabble? You don't look much like a cattle man."

"Well, I am more of someone, who tends to the business end of cattle management. I am part owner of this ranch," he said proudly.

"No, you ain't part owner of this ranch and never were, because Brantley never owned this ranch, me and my brother do. We bought it fair and square from the man that settled it originally, so it looks like any money you put into it is lost, I guess you can use it to learn a valuable lesson. Well, I guess I should carry you to the marshal, but I need to go bury my brother, so you can go, but I will go ahead and tell you, there's no need in figuring on owning any part of this ranch. I will handle it myself. The cattle will be rounded up and the brands checked. I figure most will be altered, but any that are not, will be returned to you. I will send word to you in Steamboat, when this is gonna take place," with that said, he watched Mose Dellinger walk out, mount his horse, and ride away. As he watched, he couldn't help but have that sick feeling in the pit of his stomach that he was making a mistake.

By this time, the rest of the crowd had gathered up at the house and was starting to break up and head on about their way. Only a few were left and they looked at Dave to see what was next, "Well, I guess we need to bury these fellers, probably out under that stand of trees yonder will be the best place. If someone would tend to that, I think I will go get Cabel and bring him back up here to bury. At least, that way he will be a part of the place, like he was supposed to be."

"We will bury these boys for you, Dave. Then we gotta head on back to Poole and let the old man know what is going on and what happened. We will come back, if you plan on a funeral, I am sure Mr. Hitchens would want to be here, he thought a lot of Cabel," Barrett stated as Dave walked toward his horse, it had been brought up by Bob and his guys, when they came up out of the woods.

"I'll let you know as soon as I get everything figured out. I really appreciate all of everyone's help. I will be back in a couple days."

Chapter Nineteen

Amanda was in the yard, when her father and the rest of the men rode up. She smiled a big smile and hugged Sandy, before she even realized it. She had thought a lot about him, since he had left to go to the hanging valley and had worried when she heard of the impending fight. She was just starting to realize that she had feelings for this man and that things wouldn't be the same between them now. She had known, for some time, how he felt, but wasn't sure about her feelings until now. He would have to show her that valley, for that just may be where she lives the rest of her life.

"Sandy, is it true about Cabel? Is he really dead?" she asked.

"Well, I haven't seen for myself, but according to what I have been told, it certainly doesn't look good. Dave has gone to Baggs with expectations of retrieving his body and bring it back for burial at the ranch. We have picked out a nice spot for him to rest."

Slim Montgomery rode slowly into town, fully expecting to be met by Marshal Kolb, but, surprisingly, there was no one waiting for him. He had figured that the marshal would want to discuss the happenings out at the ranch and the killing that had taken place. It was almost unnerving to him that after all that had taken place that day, three men killed, four, for all he knew, including Cabel, that the town showed no difference. Should it though? These three men were not looked on favorably by most of the population of Willow Springs, Cabel was barely known, other than by rumors and casual conversation, maybe the deeds done were only felt by those immediately involved.

His thinking was interrupted, as Kimberly stepped off of the boardwalk and ran toward him. They had talked quite a lot, but not any of the lover talk that one would expect, but there was a feeling between them that neither could deny. It wasn't spoken, only felt and that was enough for both of them, for the time being.

The fight and the stress associated with it had worn on Dave. He had fought all of his adult life in one fashion or another, but this was different and it made him appreciate what his younger brother had endured and overcome, up to this point. He had known he was still alive, when he left him in the hands of the doctor in Baggs and prayed in his heart that he would live, but, honestly, in his mind, didn't see how he could. There were cuts on his head, neck, and face, deeper than Dave had ever seen and he had lost a considerable amount of blood. It wasn't until he had him at the doctor and they started cleaning his wounds that he found out his brother had been shot and that was, also, when his hopes had faded. He still prayed for his brother's survival; but the realist in him made him prepare to take his lifeless body back to the ranch and bury him in a place where his grave could be looked after properly and visited often.

He had talked like he was already dead during conversations with others, partly to help him prepare for this moment and partly to ensure no one went looking for him to finish what they had started, but the sown side to that was that he had made himself believe, even more, that he would never see his brother alive again. He just wasn't ready for this.

Not wanting to ride in late at night, he camped outside of town to rest for the night. He had become accustom to this in a very short period and could see now what kept Cabel out here for these years. Laying on his bedroll, feeling the cool night air on his face, looking up at a million stars in the sky, *"It was a very peaceful feeling,"* he admitted to himself. The events of the day seemed to fade off into the starlit sky, as he drifted off to sleep.

Dave Glaize, ever the early riser, was up before the sun and was riding into town, just as the early morning crowd started to fill the streets on their way to whatever filled their days. Eager now, to get this business over with, he made his way up the street, past the restaurants and general stores to the doctors, and as he approached, Kristin Cross was out and about sweeping off the steps.

"Good morning, ma'am, my name is Dave Glaize and I am, unfortunately, here to pick up my brother, so I can carry him home and bury him."

'Home', he had used the word without thinking, but he guessed that would be the proper word now. It sounded pretty good, too.

His eyes opened to a white ceiling with wood beams. The mountain lion wasn't there, his knife was gone, and he had no idea where he was or how he came to be here. He thought back, as far as he could, but the best he could remember was he had been shot, so he crawled up to the cave and then the cat. He remembered feeling his knife sink to the hilt several times and the cat kept fighting. He remembered the pain from his side, as he fought, and he could feel the cuts, as the cat fought him, but he couldn't feel the pain from that. He remembered the fear that he was dying, alone, in a cave, that few people knew of or frequented. Then he could remember when the cat stopped fighting and the full weight of the animal fell upon his broken, bloody body. He remembered being tired, so tired. His arms would barely move and he could barely breathe. He could remember tasting the blood, as it ran down his face from the cuts on his head, but he couldn't raise his arms to wipe it away. Then, nothing, not darkness, not sleep; but nothing, until he opened his eyes here. He knew he was alive, the pain made sure of that, but where he was or how he came to be here he had no clue.

"Well, I see you're awake, I'll go get the doctor," the speaker, he couldn't see, until she got up to walk out of the room, was a beautiful young lady, tall, for a woman, with light brown hair and blue eyes. *"She was,"* he thought, *"One of the most beautiful women he had ever seen."*

"My name is Kristin, I'll be right back," she said with a smile, as she walked out and, suddenly, he seemed to feel better.

Opening the door, she leaned out and spoke to someone he could not see, and in a few minutes, a man came in smiling, "We didn't expect you to wake up so soon. Actually, to be honest, we didn't expect you to wake up. You have been through a lot, my friend. It's a small miracle you survived," the doctor stated, as he entered the room and sat down next to the bed.

"How long have I been here?" Cabel asked, as best as he could. His voice was raspy from the wounds and he was having problems getting the air to come out of his lungs to make the sounds.

"Four days, you have been here four days. You don't remember anything? You have been following a few commands, but this is the first time you have opened your eyes or woke up on your own."

"No, I don't remember anything. Where am I?"

"My office in Baggs, you don't remember arriving here either? Your brother brought you in, you were hurt bad, still are in bad shape, but this is a very positive sign. You're very lucky to be alive."

"My brother?" Cabel thought to himself. He didn't say it out loud for talking was painful and getting even more so, as he talked. And he wanted to save what he could for the tall nurse, when he had the opportunity. But what would she see in him? She barely knew him, if she knew him at all, for he had been unconscious, since arriving here. And, now, he would have an abundance of scars, and some would be fairly nasty, he assumed, for some of the cuts left by the lion were deep, he could remember that. Reaching up, he felt of his face and realized most of his face was bandaged as well, so what looks he may have had before, if any, would be changed as well.

Left alone now, he drifted off to sleep with dreams of light brown hair and blue eyes, mixed with nightmares of the attacking mountain lion, in some far-off dark world that he hoped he could someday forget. The ranch and the Brantley's were the furthest thing from his mind, as he lay there, but the doctor had said his brother had brought him in, that means Dave had made it, and, now, he also worried about Dave and how he would fare with the trouble going on. He smiled a little, as he thought about the results, if the Brantley's brought the fight to his brother, for he, himself, had a temper, but Dave was able to go to a different level all together.

When Cabel opened his eyes next, he was looking into the most beautiful face he could ever remember seeing. It took him a minute to focus, elsewhere, but, finally, he noticed the other person sitting at his side. It was his hero, as a kid, and now the man that saved his life, his brother, Dave Glaize.

They talked for a time, with Dave explaining how he came to find him, and what all had taken place, since he was hurt. He told him about the herd that had made it to the hanging valley and about the fight with the Brantley's. It was good for the brothers to be together again, especially, knowing how close they had come to not ever being able to talk again. But, eventually, Cabel grew tired from his wounds, so Dave had left with the promise to return in a few days.

Outside, the town was starting to move, as everyone was out and about tending to their business. They could hear the conversations taking place out on the boardwalks and in the street. There was one voice though, above all others that was familiar, but couldn't place. He searched his clouded mind for the answer, "Yep, this is bad country for snow," the voice said to someone and that was all Cabel needed. He knew who it was, it was the man who had shot him, but this time, he recognized the voice, it was the voice of Mose Dellinger. Now he knew, he would heal up, he would find Mose Dellinger, and he would kill him.

CPSIA information can be obtained
at www.ICGtesting.com
Printed in the USA
BVHW040939010820
585222BV00016B/783